7/08

W9-DCX-227

WITHDRAWN

FORT RECOVERY PUBLIC LIBRARY

THE DOVE

Other books by Carolyn Brown:

Love Is
A Falling Star
All the Way from Texas
The Yard Rose
The Ivy Tree
Lily's White Lace
That Way Again
The Wager
Trouble in Paradise
The PMS Club

The *Broken Roads Romance* Series:

To Trust
To Commit

The *Drifters and Dreamers Romance* Series:

Morning Glory
Sweet Tilly
Evening Star

The *Love's Valley Historical Romance* Series:

Redemption
Choices
Absolution
Chances
Promises

The *Promised Land Romance* Series:

Willow
Velvet
Gypsy
Garnet
Augusta

THE DOVE

•

Carolyn Brown

AVALON BOOKS
NEW YORK

© Copyright 2008 by Carolyn Brown
All rights reserved.
All the characters in this book are fictitious,
and any resemblance to actual persons,
living or dead, is purely coincidental.
Published by Thomas Bouregy & Co., Inc.
160 Madison Avenue, New York, NY 10016

Library of Congress Cataloging-in-Publication Data

Brown, Carolyn, 1948–
   The Dove / Carolyn Brown.
        p.   cm.
   ISBN: 978-0-8034-9907-2 (acid-free paper)
   1. Texas—Fiction.   I. Title.

PS3552.R685275D68 2008
813'-54—dc22

2008005926

PRINTED IN THE UNITED STATES OF AMERICA
ON ACID-FREE PAPER
BY HADDON CRAFTSMEN, BLOOMSBURG, PENNSYLVANIA

To Linda Cole,
with much love.

Prologue
Summer, 1898

Clods of red dirt fell from Katy Lynn's slim fingers and made a hollow noise as they hit the wooden coffin at the bottom of the six foot hole. She would have liked some kind of singing, but bawdy singing from the local taverns didn't seem fitting. No doubt about it, Jesse Logan would have come back from the dead to haunt her if she'd sung a Sunday school hymn at his funeral.

A daughter should weep when she buried her father. There should be mournful music, a preacher to pray over the grave, and fluttering white handkerchiefs to catch the tears of the faithful friends and relatives. But Jesse didn't have fancy words or women weeping into their little lace-edged hankies. All he had was one child and one old, devoted friend to send him on his final journey. Both wished him a peaceful eternity as they laid him to rest with other members of his family in the private Logan cemetery.

Katy's mother was on one side of him, the grandfather Katy had never known on the other.

Katy was grateful for Andy, standing three feet behind her with his worn cowboy hat in his hand. He'd been a surrogate father/mother/friend/brother/uncle all rolled into one since she was born. He was the only stable force in her entire life, and if it wasn't for him and Joshua Carter, she would be lost. At least he and Josh were dependable and would see her through the tough days ahead. The three of them would form a three-corded rope—entwined all together and making one solid force, they'd survive. Andy had never let her down, not one time. He'd been a fortress in the midst of the wild storm created by her parents when she was a little girl. When her mother died, he hadn't abandoned the fort, either. She didn't have a doubt in the world that he wouldn't be there to help her through this difficult time.

She heard a horse approaching and her heart skipped a beat. A flash of white and brown through the trees and a soft whinny let her know that Josh hadn't disappointed her. Now, Joshua was here and even though her day was as bleak as the gray sky, love surrounded her. Enough to get her through the difficult days ahead, enough to keep her sane.

Andy looked up from his bowed head and raised a heavy red eyebrow.

"It's Joshua. The guy I've been talking about all summer. I want you to meet him. Maybe he can have dinner with us."

Andy nodded seriously and waited, deep in his own

solemn thoughts. Jesse Logan had been his best friend from the time they entered first grade together: two little cocky Banty roosters. Andy just barely got through the next eight years, but Jesse was smart as well as ornery. They'd hunted for treasure along the shoreline of the river; drank their first swig of whiskey on the same night; kissed the same girl the same week; and had their first fist fight, decided she wasn't worth it, and were careful to never fall for the same woman again. In 1864 they left Spanish Fort and set out to see the world. They saw a big chunk of it together and fought a passel of Yankees just as the war was winding down. After that they signed on with a cattle company moving cows up the Chisholm Trail from south Texas to Abilene. They griped about the hot summers and cold winters, but neither of them was ready to stop what they were doing until 1878 when they were in the wrong place at the wrong time. Two sticks of dynamite were thrown into a saloon by an irate wife. Andy lost an eye and part of his ear in the explosion. Jesse lost a leg.

"Joshua," Katy Lynn ran into his arms. She could feel his heart beating steadily under his shirt when she lay her head on his chest. She could bear anything with him beside her. "I'm so glad you came."

"Katy," he pushed her back. "I'm on my way out of town. I don't know how to tell you, but this is the end. I won't be seeing you or writing to you again. I just wanted to tell you in person, not with a note."

"What are you saying? I thought you'd come to help me through this funeral."

"I'm leaving," he said. "I'm on my way to Nocona right now to catch the train. I'm going back east, Katy. My father found out about us last night and he pitched a fit, and I promised I wouldn't see you again. I couldn't leave without telling you it's all over. He threatened to cut me off if I didn't break up with you. It's been decided that I'm going to Virginia to study law. I need his money so I've got to do what he says."

"Will you come back when you finish school?"

"No, I'm never coming back here. Forget all about me, Katy. It's over and done with. It was just a few weeks of fun."

Katy Lynn's heart could not believe her ears. Joshua Carter had been in love with her all summer, or at least she'd been stupid enough to think he had. Her heart twisted into a knot and her chest ached so badly she could scarcely breathe.

"I can't believe you'd do this," she whispered.

"I don't have a choice and besides . . ." He let the sentence fade out across the hot Texas summer wind. A clap of thunder in the distance heralded a storm. Katy Lynn shielded her eyes against the sun and saw a bank of clouds coming from the southwest, moving as fast as the turmoil in her heart.

"Why don't you have a choice?" Anger replaced hurt.

"You know." He shrugged.

"No, I don't. Tell me what."

"Katy Lynn, your daddy was a drunk and your mother's reputation was even worse before she died.

We've had a lot of fun together, but that's as far as it can ever go, so this is good-bye. In a few years I'll be a lawyer and you'll be . . ."

"Where Joshua? Where will I be in your little fairy tale? Will I be working at one of the local brothels or will I have a drunk for a husband with four or five kids?"

"Probably," he shrugged.

No, I won't. I'll show you, Joshua Carter. In five years, you'll wish you hadn't been so quick to throw my love away.

Tears welled up in her eyes when she turned her back to him and deliberately made herself walk slowly through the willow trees back to the edge of the river. He wouldn't see her cry and she wouldn't run like she wanted to do. She'd hold her chin up high and walk as if she could care less about Joshua Carter.

"Where's Joshua?" Andy asked.

"He's gone." A series of thunder claps covered up the sound of horse hoofs. The first raindrops made tiny wet circles on the wooden box at the bottom of the grave. Katy Lynn picked up a handful of dirt and let it sift slowly through her fingers to land on top of the coffin. "Good-bye, Daddy," she said "I love you."

Warm tears mixed with the hot summer rain—a rarity in August in north Texas—and ran down her cheeks. Katy Lynn Logan didn't know if she was crying out of anguish for the loss of her father, out of anger for the words Joshua had just said, or because of a broken heart since she'd just lost the love of her life. She might never know, but every time it rained she would always remember her soul lying in a million jagged pieces in the willow trees surrounding the tiny cemetery—that day she had buried her father and her heart left with Joshua Carter.

Andy gave her a hug and kept his arm around her all the way back to the two-bedroom frame house not far from the cemetery. She kicked her shoes off, peeled out of her jacket, and pulled on her work suit. Andy busied himself in the kitchen making lunch. She could smell chicken frying and could hear the coffee pot gurgling. Katy liked it when Andy came to the house and fried chicken. Those were the pleasant times. The times when her father and Andy talked about the good old days. When Andy had been a swashbuckling redhead with the luck of the Irish taking care of him, and Jesse had been tall, dark, and handsome and could dance all night with the pretty girls.

What on earth was Katy Lynn going to do? She was eighteen years old, the offspring of the man who had married the resident bad girl of Spanish Fort, Texas. Her mother had died when she was four years old. She'd fallen in the river and drowned one night. Jesse would never talk about Mattie, but when she was old enough to understand, Andy let her ask as many questions as she wanted. For one time and one afternoon. After that the subject was closed. Andy told her that her mother loved her, but she loved liquor more. She'd promised Jesse she would stop drinking, so she kept her bottles hidden by the river and did a lot of fishing. It was one of those nights when she was supposedly fishing that she passed out and fell in the river. And now Jesse was gone. Doc Harris said his heart played out. Katy didn't doubt his word for a minute, but she had a million other questions. Like why now?

Answers didn't fall from the ceiling of the small two-bedroom house she'd lived in since she was born. She wrapped her arms around her slim waist and hugged herself, but there was no warmth in it. Joshua was supposed to provide that, but he'd proven to be a bigger disappointment than anyone else.

She heard a buggy turn down the lane toward the house. Her heart stopped. She hoped that Joshua had changed his mind and was returning to beg her forgiveness and offer to take her away to Virginia with him. She hoped not. There was no trust, not if he could stand there and tell her she wasn't good enough for him. She didn't want to go through life with that sitting on her shoulders. No, if it was Joshua, he could go to his precious school with his father's money and when he finished that he could go to hell. She didn't want to listen to anything he had to say. She didn't want to talk to Joshua Carter. Not that day. Or ever again.

"We got company?" Andy asked. "Maybe Josh changed his mind."

"I doubt it. It's probably Miz Raven bringing a peach pie. She would've come to the funeral, but I asked her not to. I just wanted you and Joshua there today."

"Why's that?"

"Seemed like the fitting thing. Miz Raven has been my friend through the years, but she never met Daddy. I don't know. Maybe I wasn't ready to share Joshua just yet with anyone but you. Maybe there was a little tiny bit of fear he wouldn't show up." Katy picked up a slice of raw potato and nibbled on it.

"Don't look like Miz Raven's rig," Andy said from the doorway. "Katy Lynn, you'd best come take a look at this."

"Just a minute. I've taken my shoes and the jacket to my suit off," she said.

"Don't bother. I don't think it'll matter if you are barefoot." Andy moved away from the front door.

She blinked twice as she watched a man get out of the buggy and straighten the legs of his suit pants and brush back his salt-and-pepper hair with his finger tips. She'd seen Joshua do that dozens of times.

"Hello." She opened the door and stepped out on the porch.

"Are you Katy Lynn Logan?" He started at the toes of her bare feet and traveled up the front of white lawn shirtwaist, his eyes stopping for a minute on her ample bosom. He kept going, without a hint of a blush, to the question in her crystal-clear, light-blue eyes and to the thick jet-black hair she had pulled back in a chignon at the nape of her slender neck. She was a looker, but then her mother had been too. No one in town could ever say Mattie was ugly in her prime. Every young man in the area chased her; none would have taken her home to meet his momma, Thaddeus Carter included.

"Yes, and who are you?" she asked.

"I am Thaddeus Carter. I'm a preacher at . . ."

"I know where you preach and you know who I am. You've been in the general store many times," she said bluntly. Thaddeus Carter had judged her by her parents' reputations and hadn't even bothered to check around to find out the truth about Katy Lynn Logan.

"I've come out here"—his sneer made Katy feel dirty—"to make you a deal, Katy Lynn. I want you to leave town and I want you to leave my son alone."

"Oh?" She raised a dark eyebrow.

"I heard yesterday that he's been coming out here to this . . ." Thaddeus shook his head.

"This what, Preacher Carter?" She set her jaw in a firm line.

"It doesn't matter. I just found out that he's been," Thaddeus snarled, "chasing around after the likes of you all summer and I've come to offer you money to stay away from him." He laid a brown envelope on the porch railing. "There's money in there. A lot of money. I want you to stay away from him if he comes back for a visit. I want you to promise me you won't follow him to college."

"Which is where?" she asked innocently as she ignored the money.

"Somewhere up north," he said without blinking.

"Strange, I thought he was going to Virginia, Preacher Carter. Seems like that is east, not north. Do preachers go to hell for lying like the rest of us common folks?" she asked. "Do you have a paper for me to sign in blood?"

Thaddeus stuttered and stammered, "I want your word

you won't follow him to college. I want your word you'll stay away from him."

"You got my word Preacher Carter that I will not follow him and that I will stay away from him, but you don't have to pay me for it." She started back into the house.

"Oh, yes, I do." He raised his voice. "I'd move Heaven and sell shares in Hades to keep the likes of you from my son."

"And what am I, Preacher Carter?" She turned.

"You're a . . . a soiled dove." He spewed out the words like they were gall.

She picked up the envelope. "A little dirt never keeps a dove from flying, sir. And a good rain will wash anything from the wings of a dove."

"Don't you sass me, girl," Thaddeus snapped.

"You've got my word that I won't chase Joshua and I won't have anything else to do with him," Katy turned her back and went inside the house, leaving him staring after her.

Katy Lynn opened the accounts book and went over the numbers as she kept the porch swing moving gently. Black clouds hung low in the sky off to the southwest. A crash of thunder followed a streak of lightning across the sky. She could smell the rain on the way and, like always, if she shut her eyes she could conjure up a vision of Joshua with his dark hair and brown eyes. She could see every golden fleck in his light-brown eyes when he said he loved her more than anything in the whole world. But, like always, every time it rained she could also hear the cold edge of his voice saying that she wasn't good enough for him.

She shook the vision from her mind and tried to concentrate, but it was impossible. The men who designed the sign were hanging it that day and she wanted to will the clouds to stay away until the job was finished. It was the final touch, the glory of eight months worth of hard work. Katy Lynn did not want it to rain. She wanted the sun to burn away any thoughts of Joshua Carter the way he'd burned his brand into her heart forever.

The saloon was finished. A prissy white building with shiny clean windows located fifty feet in front of her house. Three staggered steps at the top gave the illusion of a roof line that could house rooms upstairs, but it was a deception. If the customers wanted women, they'd have to go into Spanish Fort and do business at one of the three bordellos still in operation there. Andy would tend bar and toss out any undesirables. She'd play the piano. In a month she hoped the saloon's reputation would be set in concrete, and everyone would know it was a proper place to buy a drink and play cards or dominoes, and not to bring a brawl.

She'd insisted on two things: a wooden porch swing on one end of the front porch to provide a place for the ladies to sit while they waited on their husbands to have a cold one. But Katy didn't expect there would be many women from town sitting on her porch. She also insisted on swinging doors into the tavern. She'd argued with Andy when he said they weren't feasible in today's world. Vandals and thieves would rob her blind.

So she'd designed the building with swinging doors that opened into an entry hall with hat racks on both sides. Big, double doors, which could be locked to keep everything safe, opened into the saloon from the foyer. If a thief wanted to steal someone's forgotten hat then he could have it.

She carried the ledger with her and went inside to see what Andy was doing. Glasses glistened in the racks behind the long bar, which was polished to a fine shine. A mirror framed in gold gilt reflected the billiard tables, poker tables, and the biggest, blackest, shiniest piano she could have shipped to Spanish Fort.

Andy came out of the door behind the bar, the one leading into his two-room apartment and she noticed that he'd trimmed his red beard and bought himself a brand-new black eye patch. "I've got brand-new jeans and a black leather vest for tonight," he said when he found her sitting at the bar, the shut book before her.

"And a white shirt complete with garters and a bolo tie with a gold slide in the shape of a horseshoe. You are going to be the handsomest man in all of Montague County. The women are going to flock in here," she teased.

"Women in a saloon?" He shook his head. "Not likely, my child. And you'll be wearing a Sunday school dress with a nice high collar, right? Nothing that would cause a brawl."

"It's a surprise," she grinned.

She'd kept her dress in reserve. Mostly, she didn't want him to see it until the last minute, so he wouldn't insist she go back to the house and put on one of her

Sunday dresses. She'd commissioned a local seamstress to make six different dresses. Tonight's was scarlet taffeta with a low-cut neck, fitted tightly to the waist with rhinestone buttons and a slim skirt.

"Everything is so beautiful. I can't wait until we open the doors and you get all dressed up in your finery." She clapped her hands delightfully. "Andy, what would I do without you?"

"You'd be in a fancy finishing school where you belong," he said.

"Now what finishing school would take me on when they found out who my parents were and where I came from? They'd be afraid to let me close to the other ladies. I'd taint them, for sure. Besides, Andy, I'm nineteen years old. I don't think they let grown women in finishing schools. This little venture reminds me of Daddy." She changed the subject. "He always wanted a saloon but didn't feel like it was a proper place to bring up a daughter. It's going to make us richer than Midas. And besides it'll be fun. You can tend bar and run off rowdies, and I'll play the piano."

"Me and your Daddy bought you all those lessons so you could play in church, not a saloon, my child," Andy said.

"Well, he shouldn't have died and left me all that money without telling me that. He didn't tell me to build a church and he didn't tell you to preach in it, did he?"

Andy chuckled down deep in his chest. "Me a preacher man. Now, ain't that a laugh."

Leaving the book on the bar, she went out onto the porch to sit in the swing. A breeze kicked up the dust in front of the saloon. She'd thought about planting grass but the horses would trample it down or eat it all. Dark clouds rolled around back to the southwest. She saw the jagged lines of a lightning bolt and several minutes later heard a distant clap of thunder. She thought of Joshua and wondered if every important event in her life would be marked with the smell of rain in the air.

She shaded her eyes with the back of her hand and smoothed out the front of her navy-blue business skirt. She hadn't taken time to change when she'd come home from the store; she was so anxious to watch them hang her sign. Any minute now Slim Wilson, his son and the men who'd made the sign for her store in town, would be arriving. She cocked an ear to one side, listening closely, antsy to get the job done before the rain started. When the buggy appeared, it wasn't the men bringing her sign at all, but Thaddeus Carter yelling "Whoa" to a team of matched horses. She watched a streak of lightning crack above his head.

"Better duck," she yelled. "You ain't home free yet. Sometimes the Big Man takes his time when he's going to spring something on you."

"Katy Lynn," he said through clenched teeth.

"Preacher Carter," she said.

"You gave me your word." He shook his fist at her.

"I have not gone back on my word. I said I wouldn't chase your son back east to the college. I haven't broken my word, sir. I have not been out of Montague

County in the last eight months. Not since the day you laid your money on my porch rail and called me a soiled dove."

"You know what I'm talking about. I wanted you out of Spanish Fort. I don't want you here when he comes home for visits. I told you to leave Spanish Fort. You knew what I wanted and you took my money. If I'd known you were building something like this sinful place with my money I would have just had you shot instead of paying you off," he snarled.

"And when I answered you I didn't say a word about leaving Spanish Fort. It's my home, Preacher Carter. I'll be here when you are long gone off to another place and another church. It's where I was born and where I intend to stay. I said I would leave Joshua alone and I have. Besides, a lady doesn't go chasing after a man. The proper thing is to wait until he chases after her."

"I should have shot you or drowned you in the river. Like mother, like daughter."

"I think that would have earned you a back seat in hell sitting on a barbed wire fence for all eternity, Preacher Carter. Murder is a sin just like lying and the Lord does not look kindly upon the breaking of His commandments."

"Who are you to be spouting off anything about the Lord?" he growled.

"I'm Katy Lynn, the soiled dove, remember?" she said. "Now unless you want some of your congregation to see you standing in the place of sinners, you'd better chase on back to your church house. You can drop down on your knees and pray for my wanton soul until you have calluses. Maybe then the Lord will forgive you for thinking about murder and for prevaricating."

"Will you never learn to respect anything holy?"

A wagon drove up to the front of the saloon before she could answer. Her sign had arrived and what beautiful timing. "My crowning glory," she motioned. "Step back, sir, and watch them put up my logo."

"You are a slattern just like your mother." He shook his head.

"Like mother, like daughter. That's what you said. But Preacher, you don't know me so you have no business blowing the bottom out of that verse in Matthew, chapter six, verse one, that says 'Judge not, that ye be not judged,'" she said. "And your money, Thaddeus Carter, did not pay for this building. Honey, what you had in that envelope wouldn't touch the price of this place. All your money paid for was the big piano, which I could have been playing in your church. I paid for it with your money and had enough left over to buy the sign the men are working so hard to hang right now. You gave me the inspiration for the whole thing." She pointed and he looked up in spite of himself.

It was a work of art. Script lettering carved into a long piece of rough cedar and hung so that it would swing when the wind blew. The first drops of rain sprinkled down from the dark clouds just as the hangers finished their job.

Katy stepped out into the rain and watched the preacher tear out of the driveway, whipping his horses to go faster. Her hair hung limply as the rain poured, but her blue eyes sparkled as she looked up at the sign getting wet for the first time.

"Absolutely perfect," she said. "It couldn't be any better. Come on out here Andy," she called from the doorway. "It's up and swinging. I love it."

Andy joined her in the rain and looked up at the sign: *The Soiled Dove Saloon.*

Chapter One
Seven Years Later, 1905

Katy Lynn dressed carefully in a red satin dress with a tight bodice and flowing skirt edged with black lace. She tied a black velvet ribbon around her long, slender neck and flipped her long, dark hair up into a twist making a crown of curls on top. After one last look in the floor-length mirror, she opened the door and crossed the pathway to the back door of the saloon. Low clouds hung in the sky, obliterating the moon, and the aroma of fresh rain wafted through the trees even though there wasn't a drop of moisture in the air. Not yet, anyway. The smell of rain still brought back memories of Joshua Carter. Katy might think she'd forgotten the old love and the pain surrounding his leaving, but once it rained or even smelled of the fresh fragrance of rain, there it was again.

"Whew," Andy whistled through his teeth. "You are

looking fine tonight. Is that a new costume? Girl, I bet you got more barmaid get-ups than Sunday dresses out there in your house."

"Thank you for the compliment; I probably do have more Soiled Dove dresses than Sunday ones, but then church is only once a week. Piano playing is six nights a week. Get ready to be busy, Andy. It's Saturday night. Everyone has wild oats to sow." Katy grinned, but it didn't reach her eyes. Not that night. Not after letting the past sneak into her heart.

"Yep, and then'll all go to church tomorrow mornin' and pray for a crop failure. Keeps us and the churches both in business," he laughed.

She pulled out the piano bench and warmed up with "And the World Goes on Just the Same." She finished the song and went straight into "Wait 'Til the Sun Shines, Nellie."

She could relate to the tunes with no effort at all. The world had not stopped just because Jesse Logan died or Joshua Carter broke her heart; the sun most certainly had come out again after the rain, just like it would tomorrow morning. In the past seven years, she'd had the opportunity to go out with a few men, but when it came right down to the wire, she measured every one of them by her first love, Joshua Carter, and it wasn't fair to them or to her, either. She'd sent for the sheet music to a brand-new song and hummed the words as she played. In spite of working all day, plus six nights a week at The Soiled Dove, she still had lonely moments. Times when she would like to kick off her shoes, throw herself down on the settee, and share the day's events with a husband.

The doors opened and four regular customers bellied up to the bar. Andy filled tall glasses with draw beer and they carried them gently to the table where a poker deck waited in the middle. The first month she'd been open she set down the rules and few of them let a single drop of beer fall from their glasses on to the shiny hardwood floor anymore. She waved back at them when they lifted their beers in a toast to her playing and pulled the sheet music out for "And the World Goes On Just the Same." She'd probably play it several times that night just because of her mood.

Yes, the world went on year after year, but she would probably still relive that horrid event on rainy days even when she was a hundred-and-ten-years-old and couldn't remember anything else. She chose something spicy to pound out next and the four men, already into a poker game, kept time with their scuffed-up work boots. The door opened again and a couple from Nocona hurried inside. They were Saturday night regulars, who loved to shoot pool and dance. They waved in her direction. While they waited for competitors, they scooted around the dance floor in a fancy waltz. The woman's mother would dig her own grave and fall backwards in it if she knew where her daughter went on Saturday nights and with whom, but the world was changing even if it did go on just the same. Someday women would have the option of going where they wanted without the judging that went along with it.

By 10:00 the saloon was packed and Katy Lynn stood up, stretched her tight limbs, and took a break. She nodded for Andy to start up the Victrola: a new machine she'd brought in recently to give the patrons music when she wasn't at the piano. Songs were played on a 78 rpm record and Katy had every new one that was produced shipped directly to her. Andy chose one with fast playing tunes and went back to polishing glasses. The dance floor filled up with people. That record played down and he cranked up the Victrola and put another one on, to give Katy Lynn a break.

She circulated through the crowds, laughing with Jed and Martha at the pool tables, stopping to sit a while with a group of poker players. She threw her head back and laughed at one point, and Andy was reminded of Jesse. The night before the accident that almost claimed both of their lives he'd laughed like that. But what was then and today Andy had other things to think about.

He glanced at Katy Lynn again. She was the image of her mother, only softer somehow. Mattie had been a hard woman her whole life, and Andy tried to talk Jesse out of marrying her right up until the minute Jesse said "I do," in front of a courthouse judge. Five years later they buried her in the Logan cemetery not far from the house Jesse had had built with the money saved when he and Andy were on the trail. Most of it he'd gotten by gambling, not punching cows.

"Miss Katy Lynn, I just love it when you wear that red dress and play for us," a tall, lanky rancher said. "Makes me feel right good."

"Oh?" Katy cocked her head to one side.

"No offense, now." He picked up his mug of beer. "I just like the way I feel here at The Dove."

"Thank you." She patted him on the shoulder and made her way to the bar. "Andy fix me up a big iced tea with double lemon."

Andy nodded and reached for a glass. He was proud of Katy Lynn. She'd proven her mettle in business, in self-control, in self-will. If he'd married and had a child, he would have wanted a daughter exactly like her. Everything she touched had turned to pure gold. She had bought a hotel in Nocona and the money rolled in from it. She invested in another hotel out in Mineral Wells, Texas, and the profits made his head swim. She and her two friends from childhood had set up a partnership when they bought the general store in Spanish Fort back when they were only eighteen years old, right before Jesse died. Everyone in town thought he owned the store and employed them to work there, but Andy knew their real worth and just how far reaching it went. Within ten years the three of them would be the richest women in the great state of Texas if they kept up the pace they'd set for themselves.

Of all that, Andy was proud enough to burst the buttons on his suit, but the thing that really made him happiest was the fact she didn't drink. Not like either of her parents. "It's not for me, Andy," she said when they opened The Dove. "It killed my mother and ruined Daddy's health. I'll sell it, but I don't intend to drink the stuff."

She winked at him from the end of the bar and headed back to the piano when the last record ended. She chose an older slow song and two couples began a country waltz around the dance floor. It wasn't a bad life she'd carved out for herself in the past seven years. No, the three of them were doing all right for themselves. Livvy, Marie, and Katy—friends since they were six years old, now business partners as well as best friends. She lost herself in her music, but somewhere in the distance she heard thunder rumble and the old memories came back. Joshua, his eyes full of love as he toyed with the damp curls tangled up around her face after a late evening swim. A hot summer wind blew across the water and brought the smell of muddy water with it. Three things would always bring him to memory: the smell of river water, the lotion he splashed on his face after he shaved, and rain. It didn't have to be a thunderstorm or even a downpour, just the scent of rain. Her heart would twist itself into a double knot, and she'd have to remind herself to breathe. Tears would well up in her eyes and for a few moments, until she got control of her emotions, she could actually envision him standing before her.

She tried to shake the feeling from her heart, but it held on with a death grip. Every song reminded her of him. Every whiff of some old cowboy's Saturday night shave. It wasn't fair. This had been going on for seven years and Katy was twenty-five years old. Already an old maid by most people's standards. Some of the women she, Livvy, and Marie went to school with already had a houseful of children. She remembered what Joshua had said about her living in a shack and having four or five kids by now. For a minute, she almost wished she did. At least there would be someone in the shack to love her.

Joshua rubbed his square chin and combed his hair with his finger tips. It had been seven years since he'd left Spanish Fort. He thought about that summer in his life often, but most of the time it was as if it had been a dream that hadn't really happened. His mother told him after the accident that he'd cried out for several days for Katy Lynn, but he'd never told her about the young girl whose heart he'd stomped into the dirt. He remembered the harsh, unkind words he'd said to her and a slow heat rose from his neck. Returning to the area must have brought it all back so clearly—the light perfume she wore that day when she hugged him so desperately. Their hearts beating in unison as she lay her head on his chest. Seven years, and suddenly it felt as though it all happened just yesterday.

He drove the one-horse buggy down the main street in Spanish Fort. Was she still there in the same house south of the Red River? Most likely she had five or six kids hanging on her dress tail and the house had gone to ruin. Her hair would be a mess and her pale-blue eyes would have lost their luster in the daily battle of trying to make ends meet. She was probably forty pounds heavier and had twenty years worth of wrinkles etched into her face.

He'd broken all ties, even with his friends, so there was no one to see . . . except maybe Katy Lynn. Suddenly he wanted to see her. He needed to see her. Just to satisfy his curiosity. Just to prove that he'd been right. It could be weeks before he accidentally ran into her on the street or saw her at the general store, but he would see her someday if she was still in the area.

The town had shrunk in the past seven years. It had already started to decline when he was a teenager. When his father, Thaddeus, first came to the church in Spanish Fort there were two newspapers, the Burlington *Times* and the Spanish Fort *New Era.* In those days there were four hotels, several saloons—including J. W. Schrock's Cowboy Saloon, where cattle men gathered up to drink and swap stories—and several brothels. It was where Herman J. Justin founded a boot company, which had long since moved to nearby Nocona.

Joshua had heard his father preach hellfire and damnation against the brothels, as well as the saloons, in town many, many times. By the time Joshua was old enough to remember, the town was pretty much like all Texas border towns. A little rough on the edges, especially on Saturday night, but not like it had been during the cattle run days when it was said on one particular Christmas morning three men were killed before breakfast, and thirty deaths a month was pretty much the norm.

He drove south toward the river, promising himself he would just look down the lane in the direction of the house. If there were no lights, he might park in the driveway and walk down to the edge of the river where they had met every day that summer. If the house was all lit up, he'd know she might still live there. A cold knot filled his heart thinking of her being married to another man, bearing his children, washing his clothes. He tried to shake it off, but it was impossible. It was crazy to think that Katy Lynn would still be single after seven years.

He pulled up on the reins and came to an abrupt halt in the middle of the road. Where did that building come from? The moonlight lit up a sign swinging gently in the night wind. The Soiled Dove Saloon. Someone had bought her land and put in what looked like a very prosperous joint.

She must have sold out and moved on. The ache in his chest wrung pain from his heart. He'd never know what happened to Katy Lynn now, and if he was honest with himself he didn't deserve to know. He'd cast her aside like a pair of worn-out shoes. Why shouldn't she move on with her life? He certainly hadn't left her a thread of hope.

He eased the buggy up to the front of the building and watched the front door for half an hour. People came and went through the swinging wooden doors. A young couple snuggled and kissed on the porch swing. Women had no place being in a saloon. Times might be changing but not that fast. What kind of woman would sit right out in public and kiss a man like that? Evidently the town had gone backwards since his father had left five years ago. A woman, and respectable from the clothing she wore, acting like that was a true abomination. Besides, didn't they know the place was haunted? The ghost of a love that had lived for a little while between Joshua Carter and his sweet Katy Lynn would always roam the banks of the Red River.

It took several minutes before he decided to actually go inside the place. Finally he pulled the brake and hopped down from the buggy. Whoever owned the place might know what happened to Katy Lynn and his mind would be eased even if his heart still hurt. "Evenin'," he said, nodding toward the young couple who stopped kissing long enough to say hello to him. The brazen girl giggled and the man nodded toward him.

The first drops of rain fell as he swung the doors open and saw all the hats lined up in rows on racks. He found an empty hook and hung his own beside them. It must be a classy joint if they didn't let men wear their hats inside. The couple on the swing rushed past him and he overheard the lady say something about beating the man for the third time in a game of billiards. What was the world coming to anyway? He took a deep, condescending breath, and pushed inside. He let his eyes adjust to the darkness until he could see several people gathered around poker tables. The two billiard tables were in use and one couple was dancing to some kind of fast music played by a pretty good pianist off in the corner. The bar stools weren't completely filled, so he chose one at the far end where he could hear the music better.

"Tea," he told the bartender who looked up at him with a question on his face.

"Need a shot of something in that to cut the sweet?" Andy asked.

"No. Swore off the stuff a few years ago. I just came in for a little information. Piano player is pretty good. Who is he?"

"He?" Andy chuckled. "You better bend your neck around a little better Mister. Anyone who'd mistake her for a man would be stone blind and crazy as a loon."

"Sorry." Joshua apologized when he saw the back of the woman in a red dress sitting before the shiny red piano. "Pretty snazzy little joint you got here. Been here very long?"

"Six years ago we opened the doors for the first time," Andy said. "You from around these parts? Never saw you in here before."

"Used to be. Left seven years ago. Surprised to see this sitting here," Joshua said.

"I see. What would you be doing here? Anybody coming this way has to be coming to The Dove since the road stops right here. River across to Oklahoma is just through the trees." Andy set a glass of tea in front of the man.

"I'll be living here again. I used to fish in the river and wanted to drive through the whole town," Joshua explained lamely.

"Uh-huh," Andy muttered and went back to wiping down the bar.

A prickly sensation started at the back of Katy's

neck. It was simply the rain reminding her again of a lost love. That's all it could be. Joshua Carter was the past. The future wasn't hers to see. The present was right now and Joshua was not a part of it. She set up the sheet music to "Can't You See That I'm Lonely," and tried to concentrate on the intricate note procession.

Someone opened the doors and a waft of fresh rain scent mixed with the aroma of Joshua's shaving lotion floated across the dancing bodies to her nose. It was a heady feeling, but she reminded herself that the after-shave was sold in all good stores, even hers, and the cowboy who'd just walked in the door probably wore it also.

Instinctively she looked closer. No, the man silhou-etted against the open door was short with balding blond hair. He wore a dirty-blue shirt with a black leather vest. Not even in seven years would Joshua look like that. She focused on the music and inhaled the last dregs of rain and musk mixture. Next week she was going to go out with the first man who walked through the doors of Spanish Fort General Store and flirted with her. And that was a promise, not a threat. It was time she laid old ghosts to rest and got on with her life.

Andy filled a few more glasses as he made his way back up the bar. The stranger watched Katy Lynn in the mirror as he sipped his tea. Andy wondered what had happened to make him stop drinking.

"So how long have you been here?" Joshua asked when Andy swiped the bar in front of him.

"Like I said, six years."

"Did you know the folks who owned this land before? Name of Logan, I think," he asked.

"Why would you want to know?" Andy cocked his head to one side so he could see the stranger better with his one good eye.

"No reason. Just went to school with the daughter of the man who lived back down the lane a little way. Least there used to be a lane. Looks like this place takes up most of it," Joshua said.

"Yes, it does. The house is still back there," Andy nodded. "Built a covered pathway between it and here, it's so close."

"I see," Joshua nodded. "Guess you didn't know the people then."

"Didn't say that, did I?" Andy said. "Jesse Logan was my best friend in the whole world. We were friends from the first day of school when my granny and his granny took us up to the school and enrolled us. Neither one of us had any parents to speak of, so we kind of took to one another. Finished up the war together and ran cattle until he lost a leg and I lost an eye. He died about seven years ago."

"I remember," Joshua said just above a whisper, not knowing whether he wanted the answer to the next question. "What happened to his daughter?"

The music stopped.

"Well, now, did you say you went to school with her?" Andy moved down the bar to crank up the Victrola. "Back in a minute."

Katy Lynn picked up her empty tea glass and searched the bar until she found Andy at the far end. Someone was sitting on her customary stool with his head down, staring at his drink. He looked vaguely familiar, but he had to be a green horn who'd never been in The Dove because all the regulars left the stool open for Katy when she took breaks. She caught Andy's eye and held up her glass as she crossed the floor, her high-heeled shoes making little clicking noises as she weaved through the tables.

Joshua looked up into the mirror and watched the tall beautiful woman leave the piano. She looked a lot like Katy, moved just like Katy Lynn . . . catlike and graceful. But this woman had a confidence in her walk that Katy didn't have, and her hair wasn't as long. He went back to sipping his tea and wondering what the man with the eye patch could tell him when and if he ever got around to coming back down where Joshua sat. He looked up into the mirror and saw the piano player stopping to talk to the woman who'd been kissing the man on the swing. They were apparently old friends because they laughed and conversed comfortably.

Birds of a feather, like Father always said. I shouldn't be here. As soon as I find out what happened to Katy, I'm leaving. This might have clean floors and sparkling glasses, but it's just a den of iniquity.

"Hey, Katy, this fellow has been asking questions. Maybe you'd like to answer them," Andy said when she was just a few feet away. Joshua spun around on the stool, just a foot from Katy Lynn Logan. Her hair was piled on top of her head—that's why it looked so short from a distance. She was so beautiful, it took his breath away.

"Hello, Joshua," she said when her tongue became unstuck from the roof of her mouth. "It's been a long time."

"Yes, it has." He nodded. His father had been right all along. She might be dolled up in a fancy dress, but she was just a barmaid. Even if it was a classy saloon with a fancy name like The Soiled Dove, she had followed right in her father's footsteps and wasn't anything but a glorified version of her mother.

"Hello, Katy," he said.

"Tea, Andy. Leave out the lemon, please." She handed him the glass.

"How much?" Joshua asked Andy, holding up his glass.

"It's on the house," Katy said.

"Thank you," he replied tersely.

"Didn't you know you were coming into my business? You look surprised," she said.

"Your business?" He took another long look at the saloon. So she'd actually found the money to build something. Or else she'd married the old man behind the counter and it was really his bar.

"Yes, her business," Andy said "And a fine business she's built out of it, too. Respectable."

"Respectable," Joshua snorted. "He was right. My father was right about you all along, Katy Lynn."

"I think you better leave, Josh." Her voice was barely above a whisper, but it carried a cutting edge that left no room for argument.

"I think I better," he nodded. "Curiosity just got the best of my better judgment, Katy Lynn."

"You always did have a weakness in that area, Joshua Carter." She looked him right in the eye without blinking.

"Good-bye, Katy Lynn. Thanks for the drink and the music. You really do play well." He would leave with dignity. "I never knew you played or did you learn in the past few years?"

"There are lots of things about me that you never knew, Josh." She held her head high. "Andy made sure I had piano lessons from the time I was five years old. I also took ballet and art lessons for a year."

"But." He couldn't believe what he'd just heard.

"But soiled doves from the poor side of the town couldn't possibly know about finer things, could they?"

"Soiled doves?" He tried to connect the sign with what she'd just said.

"Of course. Isn't that what you left behind? A soiled dove from the wrong side of the town. Good-bye, Mr. Carter." She picked up her tea and went back to the piano.

He would never know how much courage it took for her to play without even a backward glance as the door opened and another mixture of sweet night air touched by rain and his aftershave rushed through the building to the piano bench where she sat. Or how many times she had to swallow to get the baseball-sized lump to leave her throat.

And he'd sure never know that after the Dove shut down at two A.M., she took her old patchwork quilt to the edge of the river and sat surrounded by memories until a bright orange ball brought the dawn of a new day.

Chapter Two

Prissy red roses that climbed up the porch posts along with the flower beds of yellow lantana, multi-colored petunias, and marigolds in a wild array of blossoms vied for attention that morning. Katy Lynn blinked the last of the sleepiness from her eyes and sipped her morning coffee as she kept a rhythm in the porch rocking chair. She managed a weak smile when she noticed the flowers, but it didn't last long. Her mother liked flowers and Jesse insisted even after her death that the flower beds were full every year. She wondered what Mattie might have been if she'd had the chances in life that Katy Lynn had known. If there had been an Andy in Mattie's life, would she have been a different person? The coffee had no taste and it was as cold as the inner core of her heart, so she tossed the remainder out into the yard, careful not to let it get on the flowers.

She sliced a thick chunk of bread and toasted it on an iron skillet, but the bread was nothing more than compressed sawdust as she bit off chunk after chunk and forced herself to swallow until it was all gone. Joshua Carter might breeze into her saloon just to insult her again, but he wasn't going to affect her life like that. "Well, maybe he will, but I'll be hung from the biggest willow tree on the river's edge if I don't fight it every step of the way," she muttered as she began her morning ritual.

She brushed her long, black hair and held it at the nape of her neck with a wide chignon net. She tossed the red silk kimono-style robe on the bed and opened the closet doors, choosing a pin-tucked white lawn waist with a collar of Valenciennes lace, a blue pleated skirt, and matching jacket with jet buttons. The morning was warm so she would shed the jacket of the suit as soon as church services were over. She slipped into a pair of comfortable leather shoes, tied the laces into neat little bows, and picked up her purse from the credenza in the foyer before she walked out the front door.

She hummed a hymn as she drove the buggy south toward town. She hoped Mr. Howard delivered the message that morning. He had a deep baritone voice and he usually kept her attention through the worship hour. The new minister should arrive in the next couple of weeks—least that's what she had overheard the previous week. He was in for a severe cultural shock if he'd been used to big city life. Katy didn't really care if the new preacher had an adjustment problem. She just hoped he had a big, deep voice and a good message, one that kept her on the edge of her seat for the half hour of preaching. She checked the time on her lapel watch as she went through town. Mercy, what had happened? Granted she'd had been lollygagging along, reining back the horse as she thought about the new pastor, but now she was going to be late. At least she would only miss the first hymn, but that alone was an aggravation because the music was her favorite part of the morning worship.

She snapped the reins and the horse began to trot, covering the last few blocks much faster. She stopped the buggy under a shade tree and flipped the reins around a low hanging branch, then hurried to the front door which she opened just enough to ease inside. The congregation was singing "Abide With Me," as she slipped in and slid into a back pew. She opened a hymn book and sang the last two verses, the words and melody bringing peace to her heart.

Mr. Howard stepped up behind the pulpit and Katy Lynn started to put the hymn book back in the slot on the back of the pew in front of her when she caught the edge of the book in her purse strap, dumping everything on to the seat beside her.

Thank goodness it didn't dump on the floor. That would have made even more noise, she thought as she gathered up everything and stuffed it back inside.

"We are so glad he has arrived a full week earlier

than we expected," Mr. Howard was saying when she noticed a penny on the floor. "Frankly I didn't have any idea of what message I could bring this morning. Just like writers get writer's block, I'm afraid this deacon has a preaching block."

A few people chuckled as Katy Lynn retrieved the penny.

"I'm sure we'll do our best to make him feel at home." She listened as she made sure the hymn book was secure and her dark-blue velvet purse snapped.

Apparently the new minister had arrived. She looked up just as Joshua Carter took his place behind the podium. Her heart missed at least two beats before it raced with a head of steam like a locomotive engine. The palms of her hands were clammy and she was afraid to blink for fear he'd see the motion and find her as he scanned the congregation. The dimple deepened in his right cheek as he smiled out at the people facing him.

"I'm glad to be here this morning," he said. "This is the end of a promise I made a few years ago. I made God a promise and He's come for my word. Almost seven years ago I left Spanish Fort and went back east to study law. I wanted to be a lawyer, but my dad, who's a preacher, had his heart set on me following in his footprints. Most of you will remember my father, Thaddeus Carter, who preached in this church for many years. I was eighteen that year and there was no way my restless soul was having any part of preaching. I wanted to do anything in the world but preach. You've all heard about the preacher's kid being the worst in any lot.

Well, here before you stands that bad child. The first year of college I got into so much trouble that they put me on probation. Just before school started the second year, I was in a terrible accident. I spent three months in the hospital and promised God I would do whatever he wanted me to do if I could walk out of that place with my own strength. My folks took me to their home near Texarkana until I could fully recuperate. God came for my word before I got back in school, and here I am today. But that's enough about me. Today I want to visit with you about forgiveness. We don't only forgive those who have sinned against us for their sakes. But we forgive them for our own peace of mind because it's not good to carry around grievances. . . ."

"Yeah, right," Katy Lynn whispered so low that only her conscience heard the muttering. He had a deep baritone voice and everyone seemed to be listening to his sermon except her. She kept thinking about the hateful remarks he made that day she buried her father and the things he'd said Friday night when he evidently lowered his standards and came into The Dove. A preacher sitting right at her bar with a drink in his hand. So what if it wasn't anything but tea? He was there in the very middle of a sinful place. Thaddeus Carter would have dropped graveyard dead with a cardiac arrest if he'd known his son entered a saloon.

Well, she didn't care if he sprouted big fluffy wings and a golden halo fell down from the church rafters to hang two inches above his perfectly combed head. He might have learned how to preach a sermon, how to hold an audience spellbound with his deep voice, even how to smile at the right time and tell a little funny tale to break the brevity, but he wasn't practicing what he preached. He didn't know one thing about forgiveness and that was a fact.

Joshua asked Mr. Howard to deliver the benediction and tiptoed down the center aisle to the back of the church where he planned to shake hands with each member as he or she filed out of the church. He'd practiced word association to learn to put faces and names together but it would still take him months to learn everyone in the church. It was packed completely full. He wondered if his father's much larger church seventeen miles down the road in Nocona had every seat full.

He wished his father and mother could have been there for his first Sunday in Spanish Fort, but that wasn't possible since Thaddeus had to preach that morning in his own church. The fact that his parents were in Nocona helped Joshua make the decision to come back to Spanish Fort. They'd moved there six months before when he was finishing his last courses in seminary. Then the church in Spanish Fort needed a preacher and it seemed to be divine intervention.

Katy toyed with the idea of leaving by the choir room door. Or seeing if one of the stained-glass windows in the side of the sanctuary would rise so she could slip out that way. Anything would beat looking right into his eyes and shaking hands with him. Or actually touching him, letting him touch her, even if it was just her hand. Why on earth had he come back to her town to preach in her church? She'd attended church services with Andy from the time she was five years old, but it was only after Thaddeus left that she'd made the move to this church. Granted, that was six years ago, but it was still more her church than Joshua's.

Oh, stop it. We're seven years down the road. We're grown adults, not teenagers. More than likely he erased me from his memory long ago—even before that accident he talked about. But Joshua Carter a preacher? That alone would shock the wings off an angel.

She was the last person in the line as he just reached out to shake hands with the next person without really looking. Not until their hands touched and the familiar heat boiled up from the bottom of his soul was he aware that she had been in attendance. He jerked his head around and for just a moment got lost in her blue eyes.

"Katy Lynn Logan." He smiled brightly, but there was a cold cutting edge in his voice. "Did curiosity get the best of your better judgment, also?"

"No, Joshua Carter, it did not. I've been a member of this church for the past six years. Check the church records. You'll find my name there."

"Oh? That's a surprise. I didn't know you attended church anywhere when we were . . ." He let the words slide away.

"Lots of surprises," she said, removing her hand from his. "Andy took me to the little church out south of town until a few years ago, so, yes, I did attend church. And I listened while I was there. Strange isn't it? You were in church every Sunday right here and I wonder how much you listened until you thought you were dying. Good-bye, Joshua."

"Are you coming back next Sunday?"

"I'll be here every week," she said. "I've seen lots of preachers come and go. I'll be here when you've found something bigger and better to move on to."

"Is that a threat?" He raised an eyebrow.

"Take it however you want," she said over her shoulder.

He watched her stop in the yard and talk to several people before she drove away. All he could think was that the saloon business must be very profitable. She looked like a respectable citizen, but looks could be deceiving and he'd be talking to his deacons before the week was out about allowing her to attend the church. Exactly what were people thinking, even in these modern times, of letting a barmaid attend their church? Thaddeus had told him just last week about a young girl who had danced at her brother's birthday party on a Sunday afternoon and been expelled from school for such behavior. Spanish Fort had always been a rough-and-tumble town, but this was too much. Yes, he would definitely have to call a meeting.

Katy Lynn drove in a daze. How had Joshua Carter been hired to preach in her church and she didn't even know it? She wanted to kick something, or maybe just slap him hard enough to leave her hand print on his handsome face. Anything to vent the anger raging like a forest fire inside her chest.

"I'm not going to church any more," she declared to Andy when she walked through the back door of the café. She found him waiting at the table where they ate every Sunday when she got out of church. It was a tradition he'd started back when she began school and Betsy Anderson told her she couldn't go to heaven because she didn't go to church. The next Sunday Andy took her to a little church south of town and to the café afterwards. It was tradition after that.

"And just what happened to make you want to leave your church?" He pushed her tall glass of iced tea toward her chair.

"Joshua Carter is the new preacher." She drank half of it before she set it back on the table.

"So?"

"So I'm not going back there to listen to him every Sunday. I'll find another church," she declared.

"Let him break your heart and now you're going to let him run you out of your church, too? Sounds like he's got a lot of power over you," Andy said quietly.

"He didn't . . ." her voice trailed off. "Okay, I was young and stupid and thought he was the right man for me. At least I've grown up enough to realize that. And he's not running me out of the church, either."

"I'm glad you've come to your senses. I didn't think you was that weak, Katy Lynn. I thought you had a good backbone. Good grief, you took the bull by the horns when Jesse died and look at the property you own besides The Dove. You could buy the church and own him if you wanted to," Andy laughed.

"I wouldn't own much," she snorted.

How in the world had she let Andy talk her into a corner? Now she'd have to go to church or else suffer the consequences.

Chapter Three

"What on earth happened to you over the weekend?" Livvy asked when Katy walked through the doors of the office located at the back of the Spanish Fort General Store. "You look like you spent the weekend in hell."

"That obvious, is it?" Katy set her purse on the file cabinet and picked up the calendar. "We've got buyers coming to purchase the hotel in Bowie."

"The men will be here to discuss it at ten and I've allotted two hours for that. Andy will be here at nine forty-five. You sit in on the meeting and we'll run the store." Livvy flipped through a folder.

"Good morning." Marie breezed into the office. "Mercy me, Katy, what happened over the weekend? You look awful."

"Thank you so much," Katy snipped. "We've got

business to take care of. Here comes Andy now. Since I look so awful maybe one of you better take care of the meeting and let me run the store."

"You'll scare away the customers. We'll have lunch next door and you'd better be ready to talk." Livvy shook her head. "Good morning, Andy. There's coffee and cookies waiting."

Katy listened to the proposals the three men made to buy the hotel in Bowie. She almost hated to sell it since it had been one of their first big acquisitions after the General Store and The Dove. But she followed a gut feeling when she bought it and now the same feeling told her it was time to sell. She tried to keep her mind on business, but it kept straying to Friday night when she saw the stranger sitting on her bar stool. Until he had looked up she hadn't even realized it was Joshua. Seven years had been good to him. A man had emerged from where a boy stood before, and the man made her heart beat even faster than the boy had. She toyed with a pencil and listened with one ear. The buyers had only haggled enough to keep their pride. She'd left that much margin to make a bargain, so the smart thing was to take their bid and start the paper work. She nodded at Andy, who winked with his good eye.

"Okay, we will accept that price," he said, "with the condition that you keep the same manager for six months. It will help you ease into the business and give him a cushion to decide whether he wants to continue or look for other employment."

"We are prepared to include a clause in the contract for the manager's job on a six month trial period. We'd like to keep the rest of the staff as well since the hotel is running so smoothly," one man said.

"Then I guess we're ready for the lawyer to take over," Andy smiled brightly. "I use Briggs Gann for legal work. He's a couple of doors down. If you don't want to make another trip, we can walk down there and see if he has time to make all this final this morning. Katy Lynn?"

She nodded.

"Why would your secretary need to go with us?" The older man with a snow-white beard and eyes set in a bed of wrinkles frowned.

"Because we will need her signature for the sale," Andy said.

No one put up an argument so they trooped up the wooden sidewalk to the lawyer's office. By noon the papers were written out, property transferred, papers readied for the gentlemen to file at the courthouse in Montague, and a check was made out to SD Enterprises. Andy was asked to sign in several places and Katy Lynn in one. That's the way Brigg always took care of the legal part. Andy was a figurehead and Katy Lynn was a primary owner with Livvy and Marie acting as copartners in SD. No one in town knew that the three ladies were SD Enterprises, and only the four of them—Livvy Byers, Katy Lynn Logan, Marie Harris, and Andy—had any idea what SD stood for. There'd been rumors that Andy named his business SD because of his friend Jesse Logan, who was a sad drunk. But on the corporate papers, SD was spelled out in full, Soiled Dove Enterprises.

"Whew," Katy wiped her brow and removed her suit jacket when she was back inside the store. "Andy said he was going home and taking a nap. He doesn't like the legal stuff, but he sure does bluff good."

"Let's go eat. I'm starving to death. I can't believe we just made that much money. Do you realize that's twice what we paid for that hotel? Of course, we did refurbish it and make it livable, but still, we've come out with a very nice profit." Livvy was already busy flipping the sign on the window from *OPEN* to *CLOSED FOR LUNCH*.

"What are we going to invest it in now?" Marie led the way out the door. "We could put it into that cotton gin in Nocona. We won't have to touch a thing to make money on that deal. It's a surefire pot of gold at the end of the rainbow. Hold it for a year and turn it over right after the cotton crop next year."

"I can't think about a cotton gin right now. Lord, it's already hot enough to fry my brains. I can't wait until fall really gets here. A few yellow leaves sure doesn't make it cool though, does it?" Katy said.

"Okay, Katy. It's time for 'fessing up. What happened all weekend? Something did. You couldn't keep your mind on business this morning. If it hadn't been for Andy, you would have let those fellows have the hotel for a song and a dance." Livvy tucked a strand of long blond hair back into the bun at the nape of her slender neck.

"I'll tell you while we eat." Sweat beads popped out on her upper lip and she fished in her purse for a hanky to dab them away. The heat bore down on her like an anvil. "Flies everywhere." Katy swatted at one determined to stick to her forehead. "Must be about to rain."

"The prophet speaks," Marie said when the first few drops blew in from the north. "Davy says we need rain. His ponds are all low. And he's pushing me for a Christmas wedding. What do you think?"

Katy sighed. Rain. There was a mental picture of Joshua when they were young, sitting on the old patchwork quilt under the willow trees, sharing all the dreams and hopes of a lifetime ahead. Another of him pushing her away on the day of her father's funeral. A more recent one of him in the pulpit, mesmerizing his congregation with a deep voice. The last to flit across her mind was the look on his face when he realized she was truly one of the tithes-paying people in his church.

"We didn't bring umbrellas, so we'd better do a little fancy footwork this last half a block or we're going to be wet," Marie said.

"I look like a club-footed gorilla when I run, but that's better than a giant drowned petunia if I don't." Livvy laughed. "Doesn't the rain smell good?" She took off in a run, with long skirt tails swishing around her feet.

"Rain," Katy said mournfully and started to trot. The sidewalk was already wet and her shoes made sloshing noises. Marie held the door open for her and Katy darted inside, but just as her wet feet hit the floor in the café's foyer, her right foot slipped.

Marie couldn't let go of the door fast enough to catch her, and Livvy was already inside the café looking around for a table. Katy's arm went out to break the fall and then strong arms cradled her body before it fell to the floor.

"Oh, my," she said with a shudder.

"Katy?" Joshua helped her back on her feet and held her waist just a minute longer than was necessary.

"Josh?" She was equally surprised to be ungracefully stumbling one moment and in his arms in the blink of a gnat's eyelash the next. "It's raining." She fumbled for words.

"Yes, and your feet must have gotten wet."

"Are you all right?" the waitress asked and checked the floor.

"My shoes were wet. I'm fine, thanks to the helping hand of this kind man," she said, treating Joshua like a total stranger.

"I believe she is." A red-hot rage filled Joshua. How dare she act like he was trash beneath her wet feet. It didn't matter if she was with respectable-looking friends. She was still just a bar maid in a common saloon and he was the minister of her church. She could at least acknowledge that he was someone she knew.

"Good, I'm glad you were there to catch her," the waitress said with a nod. "You gentlemen follow me, please, and I'll show you where to sit. You girls going to sit where you always do?" She motioned to Joshua and the two men with him.

Katy nodded. Marie and Livvy slid into their normal chairs, leaving Katy to sit where she had to look right into Joshua's eyes every time she looked up. Good grief, it was as if the rain brought him in the flesh rather than just memories of him. From then on she would stay in her house and refuse to open the front door if there was a storm cloud between Spanish Fort and the Gulf of Mexico.

"Now, 'fess up time," Marie said. "What happened over the weekend?"

Katy shook her head and frowned.

"Nope, you can't get out of it," Livvy laughed. "I'll have the fried chicken," she told the waitress who came to take their orders. "And I want a cup of coffee with two teaspoons of sugar."

"The same, only no sugar in my coffee," Katy said. "Excuse me a minute." She picked up her purse and went to the lady's powder room at the back of the restaurant. A washbowl and pitcher stood ready for use on an oak washstand. A fancy towel hung on the rack above them and a velvet covered bench offered a lady a place to sit while she checked her reflection in the mirror. If a woman or a man, for that matter, needed to actually use a toilet, there were two at the end of the lot back behind the café. Katy held her head in her hands for a few moments before looking in the mirror. She was more than a bit pale and there were definitely dark circles under her eyes, but hopefully Joshua didn't see any of that. She never wanted him to know that he'd kept her from sleeping two nights in a row, or that just the touch of his strong arms around her waist as she fell had practically given her a dose of the vapors.

She took a pencil and a piece of paper from her purse and wrote a note to the girls. She surely couldn't explain why she looked like she did or why she'd been distracted with him sitting less than six feet in front of her. Yet, she wasn't leaving. Like Andy said, she was a woman who'd carved a miniature empire out of her father's savings account. She wasn't about to let Joshua run her out of her church or out of her favorite restaurant either.

Joshua's breath caught in a gasp when she stood up and walked so close to him that he caught a whiff of her perfume. He inhaled deeply, wanting more and more, wanting to reach out and touch her hand as she walked by, wanting to lead her back to his parsonage and kiss her like he had years ago. She wore a navy-blue business suit with a white blouse that contrasted starkly with long black hair and crystal-clear blue eyes, but he wouldn't have cared if she'd been wearing that old pair of castoff overalls she donned when they swam in the muddy river water. She would always be beautiful in his eyes but never be the right woman for him.

"Pretty woman," one of his colleagues said in passing. "So do you think you'll mind driving all the way to Nocona for just two classes?"

"Oh, I won't mind. It's only one day a week and two

hours in evening for just a couple of weeks. It'll be a good opportunity to spend some time with my parents. I can go down there on Monday, teach the class that night, and stay with them and come back on Tuesday." What was it one of the women with Katy had said? Something about her weekend and 'fessing up? The two men were talking about the classes they wanted him to teach and he'd only caught fragments of the sentences. And then Katy shook her head, frowned, and disappeared into the back.

"Well, we're glad to have you," the other man said. "It's not easy to get someone with your credentials to teach a theology class to the elders of the church. Big help to us all. Ah, here come the steaks," he said, changing the subject.

Katy didn't even look down at Joshua when she breezed past him, but the slow heat up the back of her neck and the high color burning her cheeks let her know he was still sitting right where she'd left him. She picked up her coffee and sipped it as she carefully pushed the note across the table toward Livvy.

I can't say a word right now. Please don't ask me. I'll tell you what's going on when we get back to the office.

Livvy read the note and slid it over to Marie, who would have already started talking, but she had a mouth full of biscuit. Marie cocked her head to one side and frowned mockingly, yet her green eyes twinkled. "I think the man who caught you is damn good looking," she whispered across the table. "I might get my feet wet and fall into his arms if I had a chance."

"Shhhh." Katy tried to shush her at the same time Livvy nodded in agreement.

Joshua looked at his food, stared at the pictures hanging on the walls, toyed with the sugar bowl—anything to avoid looking at Katy Lynn Logan. He would overcome the desire in his heart if it took every last bit of willpower he had left. After all, he had the divine spirit working for him and he could squelch it all. Even though she dressed up decently on Sunday and everyone seemed to ignore the fact that she was a barmaid, he didn't have to keep reminding himself of what she really was, or that she was off limits. He shouldn't have come to Spanish Fort and as soon as another church made him an offer, he would be leaving.

A grin played at the corners of his mouth when he thought about what Mr. Howard's expression would be if he looped his arm through Katy Lynn's after church the next Sunday and told him that they were going out to eat lunch right there in the Spanish Fort Café. His favorite deacon would sharpen the guillotine and deliver the sentence without advice of jury or judge. Either he'd kill Joshua physically or else he'd see to it Joshua never preached in another Texas church. Preachers and barmaids did not mix. And that was a pure fact.

Katy noticed the grin and didn't know if he was agreeing with one of the men across from him or if he was making fun of her. How dare he be the condescending, holier-than-thou preacher right there in public. The waitress refilled her coffee and Katy picked up her fork. There would be many, many times when she would run into Joshua in the next fifty years, if she lived to be seventy-five. She stoically decided that he wasn't going to affect her like this.

Not ever again.

She shoved mashed potatoes into her mouth. They had absolutely no taste. She poured gravy on them, added salt and pepper, and tried again. They had warmth but no flavor. "So tell me about this wedding. We've been expecting it for more than a year. Why is Davy getting so antsy?"

"He wants at least five children and I'm already twenty-five. You know what they say about having babies when you're over thirty. I guess he thinks time is running out. The wedding isn't going to be anything extra big. He thought maybe we could even have it at The Dove. After all that's where we met last year." Marie smiled at the memory of her tall, lanky cowboy fiancé, who'd literally swept her off her feet. "What do you think? Maybe a Sunday afternoon when The Dove isn't normally open for business. What I've got a problem with is finding a preacher who'd be willing to set foot inside a saloon."

Katy Lynn's eyes shot up at the same time as Joshua's when he overheard the comment. Two gazes becoming one as they met in the middle of the restaurant, two stubborn broken hearts refusing to acknowledge the other. He raised an eyebrow and she set her full, sensuous mouth in a firm line.

"Only ever had two preachers come near the place,"

Katy said to Marie but talked to Joshua. "One on the day we hung the sign and opened for business to tell me he'd like to shoot me dead and the other just happened in out of curiosity. We'd better find you a judge or a justice of the peace."

"That would probably be best," Marie nodded.

Joshua's temper overruled his better sense, and before even realizing he was on his feet, he was standing at the end of the table where the ladies sat. "Excuse me, the noise level has lowered considerably since we first got here and I just overheard you say you're getting married." He looked at Marie and ignored Katy.

"Yes, I am," she said with a bright smile. "Probably at Christmastime."

"And you're having trouble finding a minister?"

"That's right. Davy and I met in Katy's saloon, The Dove. It's only about a mile from here and we'd like to get married there, but getting a preacher to go inside a saloon won't be easy and it is going to fall on Christmas Eve, so that's an added problem."

"I know where The Dove is. I used to live here and I'm the new pastor of the Baptist Church. I'd be honored to perform the wedding ceremony for you," he said.

Katy shook her head violently, but Marie wasn't paying attention to her. "Well, if that's not the luck of the Irish. Momma is full-blood Irish and I can't wait to tell her that I found a preacher who'll come inside a saloon. She said I was crazy as a cross-eyed loon. I'm Marie Harris and these are my friends: Katy Logan, the clumsy lady you caught a while ago, and Livvy Byers.

Will you put me down for Christmas Eve at two-thirty in the afternoon?"

"I'll put you on my calendar, Marie Harris. If you and your groom will call on me at the Baptist Church parsonage we'll set up an appointment for a couple of weeks before and go over the ceremony. You sure you want to get married in a saloon? People might have reservations about attending the wedding, your mother included."

"Oh, no, not Momma. She's said she'd go to my wedding if I held it in a cellar during a tornado. She's been afraid for years that she's going to get stuck with an old maid. It's a reflection on her, I'm sure. If she's got a daughter too ugly for a man to marry, then somehow it lessens her chances of getting into heaven."

Katy kicked Marie under the table and shook her head again, but Marie couldn't fathom why Katy looked like she was about to explode.

"Besides," she went right on after shooting Katy a dirty look across the table, "I want to get married there because it's where I met Davy. Katy had a case of head cold one night so I played the piano for her and Davy came in. Katy owns The Dove and plays a mean piano there. You ought to stop by . . ." Marie blushed bright red. "Ooops . . . I guess you wouldn't be interested in . . ." She stuttered and stammered.

"Not really," he smiled at her. He could literally feel the tension and the icy chill coming from behind him, but he'd teach Katy Lynn to act so high and mighty. He'd waltz right into her den of sin with his Bible in his hands and perform the nicest wedding she'd ever seen or heard and then he'd walk out just as resolutely. That would show her that he was above rendering judgment. It didn't matter if her friends were nothing more than duplicate barmaid queens; they were human after all. Offering his services to marry one of them might speak to them and lead them right into the front doors of his church.

"So you are the new preacher down at the Baptist Church. That's where all three of us go to church. We've been going there for six years now. Used to be all of us went to the little church down south of town, but we changed. Only my fiancé and I were gone last week to visit with his folks down in Prairie Valley. Did you go?" Marie looked at Livvy and Katy.

"I overslept," Livvy blushed. "So did you bring your wife?"

"I'm not married," Joshua said.

Marie looked at Katy with a question in her eye.

"Of course I was there," Katy said coldly. "I'm so sorry. I should have introduced you girls. This is our new preacher. Marie, you've just met," she said when Joshua turned around to find an icy glare. "They are both originally from Prairie Valley. We grew up together in the little church between Spanish Fort and Prairie Valley. Andy first took me there when I was six years old and they'd been there since birth. We've been best friends since the first time I walked through the Sunday school doors."

"I see," he said.

"And?" Livvy asked.

"And this is our new pastor, Joshua Carter. He and I went to school together when we were kids about a million years ago. He left town the same day I buried my father," Katy said. "And now if you'll excuse us, Joshua, we've got a store to run this afternoon. We all work at the General Store. I expect you'll be needing supplies and we'll see you there occasionally?" She threw her napkin on the table and slid out of her chair, careful not to brush against him when she did.

"Oh, my gosh," Marie stammered when they were outside. "That's your Joshua, Katy. Good grief, what have I done? I'll get in touch with him tomorrow and cancel. He can't . . ."

"That's why you couldn't talk," Livvy said. "First you fall into his arms and then he sits where you have to look at him. You said he was pretty all those years when we talked about him, but he just plumb takes your breath away."

"Yes, he did and he does, but I'll deal with it." Katy pinched her nose trying to ward off the inevitable tension headache. Why on earth had he volunteered his services? Just to humiliate her? "And you will not cancel, Marie. Joshua Carter can marry you as well as the next preacher. It'll be legal and stand right up in court and he's not making me run away. Not even from his presence in my saloon. So we'll have a Christmas Eve wedding complete with poinsettias and red velvet ribbon. I'll even play the wedding march on my piano for you to walk down the aisle we'll make by setting up chairs on two sides."

"Okay." Marie looped her arm through Katy Lynn's. "But we could maybe get married at ten o'clock in the morning so he'd be in church and couldn't marry us."

"No way." Katy shook her head.

"Was he the other preacher who showed up at The Dove? You mentioned two. One was Thaddeus Carter the day he came and said he would shoot you. Joshua must have showed up over the weekend. Did you know that he was the preacher at our church when you went in on Sunday?"

"Not until Mr. Howard introduced him," Katy said. "But listen, girls. That all happened seven years ago. We've all had first loves and we've all grown up since then. Let's talk about Marie's wedding instead of an old love gone to rot."

Chapter Four

Katy laced a fat earthworm on a hook and whipped the cane pole with enough force to send the worm and bobble out to the middle of the river. She sat down on her quilt at the edge of the water and watched the red-and-white bobble do a graceful dance in the gentle waves. She pulled her big, floppy straw hat down to a comfortable place on her forehead. The sun was high and her pale skin burned if she wasn't careful. Black hair, light-blue eyes, pale skin. None of it fit together. But then nothing in her life had ever agreed, so why should her physical makeup be any different? Her father should have been a local hero, giving up a leg in an accident when he threw his body over a woman and saved her life, but he never rode in a parade down Main Street. Her mother was the local bad girl who wouldn't have gotten the time of day from Jesse Logan when they were young. But when he came home a cripple, Mattie was the only girl who showed any interest in the disabled cowboy.

The only stabilizing force she'd ever had was Andy. He introduced her to the river when she could barely walk. He'd come on weekends to visit. In those days, Jesse and Mattie would be drinking and arguing, and Andy would take her quilt and toys to the river with him. Looking back, Andy had always been there in the tough times and she'd taken him for granted. It was Andy she ran to when her mother died, who helped her through her father's death, and who she looked forward to seeing every night at The Dove.

She had built the saloon from part of the savings account Jesse Logan left in her name, but she'd made Andy a full partner in the venture and paid him half of the profits every month. When she and Andy designed the saloon, Livvy and Marie offered to put up a third of the money each, but in that one venture, Katy wanted to go it alone. She had it built with an apartment for Andy in the back and convinced him to stop working for the railroad. It didn't take much begging once Jesse was gone because Andy thought he needed to take care of Katy. She sure didn't discourage that idea since she wanted him close by, so when the time came, she could take care of him.

She chewed her thumbnail, then realized what she was doing and jerked it out of her mouth and sat on her left hand. Old habits die hard. She'd eaten her nails from the day she started the first grade and left her dysfunctional home for the first time. Her mother threatened to spank her every time she caught her with a finger in her mouth. She'd sat on a chair so long for chewing them that Jesse used to laugh and tell her that the chair seat had the imprint of her bottom in it. Andy promised her the moon and stars if she'd stop. But it was Joshua who made her quit. He gently took her hand from her mouth one summer night and kissed her fingertips, until she was nothing more than a puddle of weak knees and a thundering heart. From then on when she began to bite a nail, she remembered the look in his eyes.

She shivered in spite of the summer heat, and at the same time a gentle breeze stirred the tree limbs and brought that familiar scent to her. She sat very still. If Joshua was close enough that she could smell his aftershave, she intended to make him think she could care less. Most likely, it was just a figment of her overactive imagination . . . again. This was most likely exactly what it had to be because Joshua Carter surely wouldn't be coming back to the river for anything. He certainly hadn't left anything to come back to when he rode away all those years ago and since he'd been back all he'd done was look down on her with contempt in his eyes.

A slow heat started at the base of her spine and tickled its way to the top of her neck when he shook out a blanket not six feet from her and opened a rusty, old tackle box. She stole a sideways glance at him without turning her head. Faded denim jeans, a dark green shirt with a patch on the sleeve, old boots worn down at the heels and no hat. He didn't have to worry about too much sun on his face. It was already tanned to perfection.

He combed his hair with his fingertips and baited a hook with a wiggling, fat worm. Then with the ease of lots of practice, he let the bobble fly through the air and settle on the top of the water a few yards downstream from Katy's. Two red-and-white bobbles in plain sight of each other, yet they'd never get tangled up because of the distance between them.

A lot like me and Joshua Carter. He could sit there until the next blue moon and we'd never fit together. I'm a barmaid and he'll never be interested in me again. Not unless it was like that summer when he had a need to sow wild oats. But I'm not willing for that any more. I wonder if preachers have some kind of divine intervention from heaven that keeps them from even desiring to kiss a soiled dove on an old quilt beside the river. And he is just that . . . a preacher man. Which means even if he fell off his cloud, he wouldn't ever be seen with me in public. Stories with happy endings only happen in dime-store novels, not in real life.

The red clay banks of the Washita River were free territory so she couldn't very well tell him to leave. But, oh, how she wanted to scream and yell. Childish as it might seem, she wanted to tell him how he'd broken her heart in a million pieces and how he had no right to preach in her church, eat in her favorite restaurant, and butt into her friend's life with his offer to perform the wedding. Now he was stealing her final refuge. The banks of the river was where she had fished for hours, read so many books she couldn't remember them all, and solved so many problems it would take a ream of paper to list them.

"Fish biting today?" he asked after half an hour of silence.

"Not yet," she answered. He could sit right there in the boiling afternoon sun and listen to her talk all afternoon. He wanted to hear her honeyed, slow drawl say something other than a couple of one-syllable words. She could recite poetry or read from Psalms until the sun went down, or even just tell him every minor detail of her life for the past seven years, and he'd just nod and smile. But he might as well wish for the sun to stand still because it wasn't about to happen.

"I went to the saloon and it was locked." He didn't look at her, but he didn't need to. He could shut his eyes at midnight on a moonless night and see her laughing and running through the trees toward him that summer a lifetime ago. He'd wait for her at the edge of the river and she'd come out of the willows in a dead run and literally jump into his arms.

"Hours are on the door. We're never open on Saturday afternoon." She remembered the way the moonlight flickered on the water when he held her tightly and kissed her passionately, awakening the woman inside the little girl that summer. She'd give half her fortune in SD Enterprises to be able to blink all those memories away forever.

"I knocked on the door of your house."

She didn't answer.

"I came to talk to you, but since you weren't home I

figured I'd fish a while and catch you later this afternoon," he explained. Why did she have to be a barmaid? Why couldn't she have done just what he expected and married some snuff-dipping farmer so he could get her out of his mind?

"Talk." She opened the door for him with one word, but her tone left no doubt she could and would slam it shut any time she wanted.

"Katy Lynn, I . . ." He stammered over the words he'd practiced so carefully all week. "I owe you an apology."

"For what?" She kept her eyes on the bobble in the middle of the water. Some folks said the water was bloodred, but in an artist's colors it would probably be painted in burnt sienna with just a tiny bit of white mixed in for the tips of the waves.

"You're not making this easy. Could you look at me?"

"No."

"Okay. I guess that I deserve your anger. I am here to ask you to forgive me for my insensitivity that day when I came to tell you it was over. You were burying your father."

She nodded and swallowed the lump in her throat.

". . . and I should have shown a little more kindness. I was wrong in the way I handled it. I don't know what I should have done, but it wasn't right. I was also wrong to talk to you the way I did last weekend when I realized you were a barmaid."

"Piano player. Never have been a barmaid. Andy won't let me."

"Then piano player. Will you forgive me?"

"Forgiven," she said nonchalantly.

"Forgotten?"

"Never!" She blinked back the tears. She would not promise what she could not deliver. Forget the words. Forget Joshua. That would be as impossible as Katy Lynn going on living after she stopped breathing.

"Okay . . ." He dragged out the word. "We'll have to work on that part."

"I don't think so. Sometimes it's too late to say I'm sorry and it's too late to do what you should have done all along. I'll forgive you Joshua, because I can't harbor hatred in my heart. It would eat up everything else. But I won't forget so we don't have to work on it."

"Is Andy your husband?"

She chuckled. Andy was everything but husband to her. Brother, uncle, aunt, sister, mother, father, fishing buddy, business partner. "No," she answered.

"Ever been married?"

"Is this a book about my life? I don't think this is any of your business." she snipped crossly. He'd done his penance and she'd given him partial atonement. She'd forgiven even if she couldn't promise to forget. So he could gather up his fishing equipment and go on home.

"I'm trying to make conversation, Katy Lynn," he said.

"Are you married? Are your wife and six kids just waiting to come to Spanish Fort when they get things packed up? Does she dip snuff?"

Joshua set his handsome mouth in a firm line and drew his eyebrows down into a solid black crease at the bottom of a brow full of angry wrinkles. Katy didn't miss a single nuance or gesture.

"I'm not married. Never have been and I don't think I've got six kids hiding in the woodwork. There are no kids or snuff-dipping wife."

"I'm not married. Andy was my dad's best friend. He's the one who took care of me when my folks were too busy hating each other to know or even care that they had a daughter underfoot. He's the one who took me to church and piano lessons. He made me take art lessons and ballet, but I hated both of them. He was here that day I buried Daddy. He waited for me to bring you to meet him."

"I'm sorry," he said and she believed him. "Engaged?"

"Not yet." She left room for doubt. "You?"

"I've been thinking about that step."

Her heart fell in a heap somewhere down around her toes. It might be best if he did have a fiancée—a wife to sit on the front pew and listen intently to every word of his sermon, to teach a Sunday school class and visit the sick with him. A charming little woman who never dressed up on Saturday night in red satin and fancy shoes to play the piano at The Soiled Dove.

"I'm going to tell your friend Marie that I can't perform that wedding for her." He changed the subject. "It was rude of me to offer my services like that. She can find a judge or a justice of the peace, or maybe since it's on Sunday afternoon, another preacher. I realize she is a member of my congregation and she might have even asked me to do the service for her, but I shouldn't have butted in like that. It was rude and I'm going to tell her I can't do it."

"Why did you do it?"

"Because I was angry with you," he said honestly. "You didn't acknowledge me when I caught you, then you didn't look at me when you went to the ladies' room. When you returned you were so snobbish, it made me angry. So I overheard your friend and I offered in an attempt to make you as angry as I was."

Katy suppressed a smile by biting the inside of her lip. So he'd been upset. Well, that was absolutely just the most refreshing news she'd had in days. He'd filled her up with enough anger she might go to her grave with part of it still hiding in her soul. After seven years of nothing, he'd charged back into her life like a big, mean bull, and totally wrecked havoc with the rut she'd prepared so carefully and meticulously all those years. "Don't back out on Marie. She needs a minister. You fill the bill and it won't bother me for you to do the ceremony. Unless it will make you uncomfortable to be in the Saloon."

"No, I can handle it. I just don't want to put you in a difficult position," he said.

"Joshua, we were kids seven years ago. We're adults now." She wondered whom she was trying to convince? Joshua . . . or Katy?

"That's right." He nodded.

"Your presence at a wedding surely won't bother me." She checked the sky for lightning bolts to dodge for telling such a blatant lie.

"I'm glad. Will you be in church tomorrow morning?"

"I'm in church every Sunday. Andy waits for me at the café in town and we always have dinner together. It's been ritual since I was six years old," she told him.

"He could come to church with you," Joshua offered.

"He goes to a different church," she said. "He had a lady friend when I was a little girl and . . ."

Joshua waited for her to finish but finally decided she wasn't going to offer any more information. Katy had talked his ears off seven years before. They talked about their fears, their goals, and their future. Or had they? Looking back, he suddenly remembered that he talked and she listened. He didn't even know about Andy or her church until the past week. He didn't know about her two friends . . . Livvy and Marie, both from Prairie View.

"She was a real lady," Katy picked up the story again. "She dressed proper, ate proper, and Andy thought she was the Queen of Sheba. So he sent me to church with her. She died when I was thirteen, but by then I knew how to behave in church and Andy and I had our little ritual."

"I'm sorry," he said with real feeling. Had Katy never had a single break in her life? Her mother, her father, the lady who took care of her religious upbringing . . . all dead before she was even of age.

"Thank you," she said. "I don't think they're biting."

"Doesn't look like it," he said. Somehow he felt as if the whole morning hadn't been a complete loss. She'd opened up to him a little and she'd forgiven him. That's what he'd driven to the river for anyway. To bare his soul and ask forgiveness—she'd granted that much. It probably was too much to ask for forgetfulness too. She seemed preoccupied and he couldn't see her under that wide-brimmed hat to tell what she was thinking.

Apparently she was interested in someone else. Maybe even waiting for that man to come to the river's edge to fish away the afternoon hours. That's why she was so cold toward him, but then what more could he expect. She made her living in a saloon, so she'd never be interested in a preacher. She liked the old Joshua. The one who was young, carefree, and would spit in the devil's eye. The new Joshua, born after the accident and hours and hours of therapy, both mental and physical, wouldn't interest her at all. The scar making a rubboard mess of his back and upper left arm would disgust her. Not to mention the one on his left thigh. He couldn't imagine throwing off his shirt and lying down beside her wearing nothing but jeans after a cool dip in the river.

She reeled in her line. The worm was gone. The minnows had feasted well even if the catfish she'd hoped for weren't biting that day. She picked up her tackle box and folded her chair. "Hope you have better luck than I did." It was as if she was talking to a complete stranger. Someone who just happened to be fishing beside her, not someone who one summer long ago had kissed her until she was breathless.

"I'll give it a while longer. See you tomorrow morning. Thanks for the visit."

"Sure thing." She nodded. "Like I said, we were just two silly kids. Life goes on."

"Yes, it does," he agreed.

Neither of them believed it.

Katy dressed in her black satin costume. A long, silky dress with a side slit and hot-pink roses attached to the thin straps. She'd throw a lacy shawl around her shoulders and secure it with a silver heart-shaped brooch she'd ordered last week from the Sears Catalog. She left her hair down and entwined a halo of silk roses at the top. It was the most revealing outfit she wore to The Dove—the one that made her look most the part of a barmaid from twenty or thirty years ago.

She had paced the floor until she was tired and tried in vain to nap. She had sat in a long hot bath and attempted to read the latest novel from her favorite author while she soaked, but after the first ten pages she didn't even know what she'd read so she laid that aside.

He had a woman back in Texarkana, one he'd dated and was thinking about asking to marry him. He'd said he was thinking about engagement and that had to be what he meant. He'd just wanted to clear the air with me before he brought his wife to Spanish Fort; make sure I wouldn't cause some kind of stink because of the past.

She'd talked to herself while she soaked, but her heart and mind were disconnected and her heart wasn't interested in hearing anything that would make it hurt more.

"Wow." Andy whistled under his breath like he always did when she walked into The Dove. It wouldn't matter if Katy Lynn showed up in a baby-pink Sunday school dress with accents of white lace, he'd still tell her she looked beautiful.

"You are prejudiced." She managed a weak grin just for him.

"Yep, have been since the day I came to the house that morning after you were born and you were there in a wooden box. All red and wrinkled with black hair that stuck up every which way. I was just glad you had ten toes and fingers and everything was fine. Went the next day to the store and bought you a proper cradle and all the things they had for a baby girl. Your momma should've been ready for you, but you came a little early," he said. "So what did Joshua Carter want today?"

"How did you know he was here?"

"I came to do a little fishing. Saw his horse staked out in the yard and walked a little ways down the woods. I could hear him talking and you weren't screaming or yelling like I figured you'd do when you got the chance. Thought you might like a little time to tell him how the cow ate the cabbage, so I just went on back home and took me a proper nap so I'd be ready for the night." He swiped the already-clean shiny bar one more time with a white cloth.

She leaned on the bar with her elbows. "He came to apologize."

"He owed you that much and probably a lot more. Did you forgive him?"

"Yes, I did. He wanted me to say I'd forget, but that would be a lie."

"Only a foolish man would expect that after the things he said in here. I don't know what went on when you were kids. Just that that old Preacher Carter didn't want Joshua seeing you and gave you that envelope of money. I was always kind of surprised that you took it since the boy had already broken your heart."

"Thaddeus was hateful. Comes a time when a person has to pay for their attitude. He said unkind things about Daddy and Momma, and he called me a soiled dove," Katy admitted. "And If I'd told you that day, you would have turned the fire out from under the chicken you were frying and gone hunting Thaddeus Carter with a shot gun."

"Yes, I would have." Andy nodded seriously. "So why didn't you tell me?"

"I was hungry." Her blue eyes twinkled. "And I didn't know how to finish frying that chicken. I'm going to warm up." She started toward the piano. "Joshua and I were just kids back then, Andy. We're adults now and it's all over. Don't you be worrying about anything. I forgave him. I won't forget because remembering makes darn sure I won't make the same mistake again. Besides he's a preacher and I'm half owner of a saloon. Thaddeus is still alive and kicking and he'd shoot me before he let his son get involved with me. So all in all, there's just too much against us for any of it to ever work out anyway. Besides I think he's probably about to ask some woman from where he came from to marry him. He just apologized to make sure I didn't make a big stinky mess when she arrives."

"And you are talking too much, my child. Who are you trying to convince? Me or you?" Andy chuckled.

Chapter Five

Katy noticed the leaves were finally turning as she drove to work that morning. It wouldn't be long until winter arrived. That meant rain and more rain—normal Texas winters were cold and wet. She parked the buggy in front of the livery stable and handed the reins to Mr. Bailey. He'd take care of the horse all day, feed him well, and have the buggy ready to go when she locked up for the day. She went past the café and darted in for a two blueberry muffins and a big chocolate cookie. She wondered if Thaddeus even knew she was still in Spanish Fort or if he cared. Probably when his son decided to give his life and heart to the Lord, he figured Joshua was healed of the disease known as Katy Lynn Logan.

She looked forward to a trip to Gainesville in the next couple of days. She would ride to Nocona and catch a train east where she'd conduct her business.

Andy was going with her and they would look at the lumberyard SD Enterprises was interested in buying. Someday she would be able to do business on her own. Women were beginning to stand up and yell and someday, hopefully in her lifetime, things would change. But until they did, thank goodness for Andy.

She had her mother's tendency to gain weight around her waist and she kept a close watch on the amount of sweet things that went into her mouth. But that morning she needed chocolate—a poor substitute for what she really wanted, but it would have to do. She ate half the cookie before she realized she had not enjoyed a single bite. She tossed the rest of it out into the dirt street. The birds, armadillos, or possums could fight over the remains. She thought about the song she played on the piano: "And the World Goes on Just the Same."

That's what I need. I need to have a wreath made, go to the edge of the river, and have a funeral for the love we had all those years ago. I could pick the flowers off and toss them in the river like they were ashes and when it was done, I'd have closure. It would truly be over. Stop it. She chastised herself. *You're letting him make you morbid. You stated your position a couple of months ago and he's been coolly businesslike every Sunday since. That's what you wanted, so get over it. What you need is a tall, dark, handsome fellow to make you forget him.*

Yeah, right. Forget? Nothing doing! I'd like to slap him. Or kiss him, her conscience snipped and she moaned.

She breezed into the store to find Livvy and Marie smiling like two contented Chessy cats. For a split second she thought about what they had to do that morning and came up with a blank. Nothing exciting about selling groceries. She hated surprises and the twinkle in both Livvy's near-black eyes and Marie's Irish-green ones said she had one in store.

"Okay, do I have coffee on my blouse?" She looked down at the ivory-silk waist. No, it still looked just like it did that morning when she took it out of the closet. "Something ugly on my teeth?" She ran her tongue over her front teeth.

"You've got company," Livvy said. "Mr. Howard is in your office to discuss something about the church."

"What does he need? Why didn't you just write him a check like always?" She set the muffins on the counter top. "I brought you each a muffin."

"Thank you. I'm starving even if I did eat a big breakfast. Bride's nerves, Momma says. She says if I don't stop eating, Davy will be getting two women. Oh, Mr. Howard? He didn't ask for a thing. Just wanted to wait a few minutes until you arrived." Marie was holding in a giggle and Katy knew the real surprise wasn't out yet.

"Okay, then I'll go take care of it. But you two could very easily be in a world of trouble if you know something and you're hiding it from me." She shook her finger at them.

Joshua didn't want to go to breakfast with Mr. Howard, but he didn't have a single excuse why he shouldn't. The man was his favorite elder and had been a tremendous help during the past three months that he'd been in Spanish Fort. He never missed a service or a business meeting and had befriended Joshua as a person as well as a pastor.

They had biscuits and gravy at the café next to the general store and then Mr. Howard commenced to tell him all about one of his congregation, Katherine, who had been coming to the church the past several years. "Now I'm not playing matchmaker with you, Joshua, I wouldn't do that." His hazel eyes, set in a bed of deep wrinkles, glittered. "For all I know you've got a lady friend back where you came from, but I think it's time you got to know Katherine better than just a handshake on Sunday. That's just formal. I want you to really know her."

"Katherine?" He tried to put a face with the name. He'd met lots of women, but he couldn't remember a Katherine. Perhaps she was one of those mousy types—medium height, medium brown hair, eyes of no descript color. He couldn't think of anything fascinating or even outstanding by which to remember her. Just a common face in a sea of new people he worked hard to remember. Maybe they called her Kathy and that's why he couldn't place her. He worked his brain harder, trying to conjure up a Kathy, but it didn't work.

"Katherine has been a solid pillar in the church the past few years. Any time we need something she's right there. She was a strange little girl. Came with my baby sister, Madge, back when she wasn't any taller than my knee but that was when we all went down to the other

church. She was a spitfire from day one. I taught her
Sunday school classes and let me tell you, if there was
a question about anything, she asked it at least twice.
By the time she was baptized into the church, I didn't
know if she'd taught me or I'd taught her."

Joshua drew his eyebrows down in a firm line. Surely
someone else would have mentioned Kathy or Katherine if she was helpful in the church. There was a business meeting just last week when they'd discussed the
need for a new organ, but he couldn't remember anyone
saying anything about such a woman. *She's plain and
maybe older than I am*, he finally thought. *That's it.
She's an older woman, maybe even widowed, who smiles
every Sunday and tells me what a good sermon I just
preached.*

"Katherine Lyndsey is over at the general store. If
you are free this morning I'd like to take you over there.
I won't be staying long. I need to ride over to Burlington to visit my oldest sister, Annie. She moved there to
be near her son when she fell and hurt her leg. Has to
use a crutch nowadays, but she's still just as sassy as
ever. But maybe you could ask Katherine to lunch. After all, she is your biggest financial supporter," Mr.
Howard said.

"I'll be glad to go with you," Joshua said. "I should
have visited Mrs. Lyndsey before now if she's that in-
strumental in the church. Does she own the general
store? Maybe we should have made an appointment."
He hoped Katy Lynn wasn't there that day. Maybe one
of the other ladies, Livvy or Marie, would be working

out front and he'd be spared the ordeal of dealing with his feelings every time he was in Katy's presence.

"Oh, no, I run by every chance I get. She's always got time for me," Mr. Howard told him.

Joshua had heard that Andy, the one-eyed man who kept bar for her at The Dove, actually owned the store and employed the three ladies to run it for him. Evidently he'd heard wrong because Mr. Howard led him to believe Katherine owned the store. Something surely wasn't right.

"Well, good morning, ladies," Mr. Howard greeted Livvy and Marie, who almost spit their coffee before they got control of themselves. "We stopped by to visit with Katherine. Is she here yet?"

"No, but she will be soon. She had to go to the bank and she'll be right back," Marie said. "What are you two doing out this early?"

"Just visiting." Joshua smiled.

"Mind if we wait in her office?" Mr. Howard asked.

"Go right on in and I'll bring you a cup of coffee," Livvy said. "So you're just out doing visitations?" She ushered them through the door.

"Yes, I thought it was time Joshua met Katherine and got to know her a little better. She's such a stable supporter in our church." Mr. Howard sat down in one of a pair of matched deep-blue velvet chairs and motioned for Joshua to take the other one.

"Back in a minute," Livvy said.

A picture of a young man sitting on a horse sat on an oak filing cabinet. The man had dark hair and light eyes and smiled for the camera. There was another picture beside it . . . a pretty woman with long, almost stringy light-colored hair she'd slicked up into a bun, and the palest eyes. She held a little girl in her lap. The child had the same eyes as the lady but with dark hair. There was something vaguely haunting about the child and the woman.

Joshua told himself a story about the pictures while he waited on Livvy to bring coffee. The man was a Civil War hero who didn't make it home. The woman was Mrs. Lyndsey and the little girl, her only child, Katherine, who grew up to be a bit on the plain side. Mrs. Lyndsey was a widow with gray hair these days but time was when she was a real pretty woman. Seemed like there was a woman who always sat in the middle of the church with a young lady who might fit that bill. Late sixties. Always dressed in a dark suit. A younger woman who was subdued and wore spectacles perched on the end of her nose when she ran her finger down the Bible passages.

"Cream or sugar?" Livvy set a tray on the desk.

"Just black." Joshua smiled. "So how long have you worked here?"

"Six years. Right after Katy Lynn built The Dove. She had a job here already and Andy hired us to help her out. She should be here in just a few minutes. She's never more than ten or fifteen minutes. Just has to take the week's cash to deposit it. Unless there's a line, it doesn't take the teller long to count the money."

"Thank you." Mr. Howard sipped the coffee and nodded.

Katy Lynn removed her jacket, hung it over a ladder-back chair behind the long table they used to measure fabric, and slicked back her black hair, tucking in any errant strands. She'd arrived at church the Sunday before and had overhead the ladies sitting in front of her and visiting about the business meeting. They mentioned that the church needed a new organ so that's probably why Mr. Howard was waiting in her office. He'd asked her several times to sit on one committee or the other, but she always begged off with the excuse that she didn't have time with two full-time jobs. But that didn't keep her from writing a check whenever he thought the church needed anything. He'd kept her on her toes when his sister first brought her to his Sunday school classes and she couldn't refuse him a thing when it came to the church. She smiled when she remembered how hard she studied just so she could ask an intelligent question.

"Well, good morning." She breezed into her office. "What brings you to town this morning?" Her voice started off light and happy and ended on an incredulous note when she saw Joshua stand up as well as Mr. Howard.

"I brought the new preacher to meet you in person, Katherine. I know you've shaken hands with him on Sunday mornings after services, but I thought you two should really get to know each other since you do so much for the church," Mr. Howard said. "I'm sorry to introduce and run"—he laughed at his own joke as he checked his watch—"but I promised to have lunch with my sister in Burlington and you of all people know exactly how taxing she can be if I'm late for the meal."

"Don't I?" Katy smiled.

"Quite all right." Joshua's mind was flitting around trying to find pieces to fit together. Katherine Lyndsey . . . Katy Lynn. The same person?

"See you in church next week, Katherine. Sit up tall and listen to me. It always helps to look out there and see you listening. So many folks are just sleeping with their eyes open." He patted her on the shoulder and was out the door before either Joshua or Katy could say another word.

She made her jelly-filled knees carry her to the other side of the desk and ease down into the chair. Mr. Howard didn't know that she and Joshua Carter had a history, so she couldn't blame him for the morning, but she'd sure like to kick someone. Maybe Livvy and Marie for starters. Some friends they were. They could have at least told her she was walking into a rattlesnake's pit.

Joshua noticed another picture sitting on her desk. The bartender in the saloon, the man with the black patch on his eye, and Katy Lynn. She wore a business suit and Andy smiled into the camera, pride written all over his face. If he'd seen that picture first he would have realized who Katherine was and his heart wouldn't still be chasing around in his chest like a hound after a coyote.

"So how long have you worked here?" he finally found enough breath to ask.

"Few years." She picked up a pen and toyed with it.

"I didn't know your name was Katherine," he said.

"Katherine Lyndsey Logan. Lyndsey after Momma's maiden name. She was Mateline Lyndsey before she married Daddy. Katherine after Daddy's grandmother. Andy said it was too much name for a baby so I was Katy Lynn from birth. Only Mr. Howard insisted on calling me by my real name when I started church." She said too much, too fast and wanted to bite her tongue off at the root. He'd think she was nervous and she wanted to leave a cold, impersonal effect on Joshua every time she was around him for the rest of her life.

"I see. I didn't know who Mr. Howard was talking about or I would have declined the offer to come visit with you."

"I'm sure you would have," she said.

"What is SD Enterprises?" he asked, motioning toward the script lettering on the door.

"It's a business. We buy floundering businesses, build them up, and resell them. We also invest in new companies to get them on their feet and then bow out when the profit is right," she said.

"And you're a secretary?"

She smiled. "Something like that, I guess."

Livvy knocked on he door. "Miz Raven is out here with Susanna. She says you know something about a piece of fabric she ordered?"

"I do," Katy said and stood up.

Joshua was mesmerized by the picture of her and Andy. Looking back, he knew he'd made a terribly wrong error in judgement. "I'm sorry. I was looking at that picture," he said, awkwardly standing up and making his way to the door. He followed her out and looked around the store, trying to decide if he needed anything.

"Miz Raven. How delightful to see you and Susanna today. I do remember that fabric. I put it under the counter just in case you decided you might need more. And by the way, I'm going to Gainesville to look at more stock this afternoon. Would you like me to pick up some blue velvet? I know how partial Susanna is to it in the wintertime."

Joshua shoveled beans into a brown paper bag and accidentally brushed against Katy's shoulder when he passed her at the fabric table.

"Pardon me," he said.

"Yes, sir," she said without looking at him.

"Secretary?" he whispered. "You must be some high-powered secretary to do that kind of job."

"Something like that." She smiled, but it didn't have any warmth to it.

"Can I take you to lunch? Mr. Howard has convinced me that you are the mainstay of my church and I'd like to at least express a little appreciation," he said loudly while he tried to digest the fact that Katy Lynn was a whole lot more than a piano player in a saloon on the south side of the river.

"I'm sorry." She remembered giving Thaddeus her word that she'd stay away from Joshua. "I really don't have time and besides you really don't want to take me to lunch, Joshua. Mr. Howard, bless his little heart, didn't realize what he was setting up. It wasn't your fault. But . . ."

"I understand." His heart was suddenly a lump of stone in his chest, and confusion filled his soul. She was the owner of a glorified saloon and his deacon thought she hung the moon. Didn't Mr. Howard know what she did after she left the general store every evening? If he did, he would be ready to roll her in hot tar and chicken feathers and ride her out of the church on a rail.

Nervous energy filled her insides. She wanted to crawl over the table and kiss him until she was breathless. She wanted to pick up the scissors and thrust them toward his pretty eyes. She wished he would disappear. She wished he would insist she go to lunch with him. Nothing made a bit of sense.

"Who is SD?" He didn't disappear but stayed right beside her even while Livvy rang up the sale of the fabric to Miz Raven and her daughter, Susanna.

She didn't know how much longer she could stand him being there.

"Thank you, Miz Raven. I'll have that velvet in here by the end of the week. You and Susanna have a lovely day," she told the lovely woman and her teenage girl as they began to leave.

"Just call me, darlin', and I'll be right in to get it. And when are you going to be ready for a few new designs? I've been working on a fabulous one with feathers around the neckline."

"It sounds wonderful. I'll be out to the Paradise in a few days and we'll have tea if that's all right." Katy continued to ignore Joshua.

Miz Raven raised an eyebrow and glanced his way.

Katy shrugged.

"Later," the woman mouthed.

Katy nodded ever so slightly.

"SD isn't a person." She turned to Joshua, her eyes nothing more than slits. "It's just initials."

"So what does it stand for and who does own this big business? Or is it a bunch of people and you're a secretary or something?"

"SD is a corporation. It's owned by three partners: Livvy, Marie, and myself. Since I put up the finances to begin the business, I'm the senior partner. Andy is the front man for us and if you tell a soul what I just told you I will put a bullet between your eyes. People don't sell businesses to women even if they are smart and qualified to run them. SD stands for Soiled Dove, Joshua," she told him bluntly.

"Why?"

"Like I told you before, that's what you left behind. A soiled dove. Ever seen a dove, Joshua?" She took two steps toward him and looked over his shoulder at storm clouds gathering in the sky. Had she thought about it, she would have known Joshua would bring a storm with him.

"Yes, I have," he said.

"They're as white as the driven snow. Beautiful, peaceful birds. And you want to know something, they can get smoke or dirt on their wings and it doesn't keep them from flying. You came to see me that summer and folks who knew my Momma figured there was a lot of dirt on my wings, but it didn't keep me from flying, Joshua Carter. I didn't marry a snuff-dipping farmer and I didn't move into a shanty. I made a life for myself. The Dove is a gold mine, and I invested my father's savings wisely."

He nodded, unable to say a word.

She turned slowly to face him, to look him right in the eye without blinking. "And one other thing maybe you'd better understand. I'm still the same Katy Lynn. My mother was the bad girl of Montague County. My father was a drunk, disillusioned cowboy who tried to drown his disappointments in a bottle. It doesn't matter whether I'm dressed up in a red sequined costume as the piano player at the saloon, or whether I'm sitting amongst your congregation listening to you deliver the Sunday morning message. It doesn't matter if I'm sitting before you in a fancy custom-made suit making plans to go to Gainesville and buy a lumberyard right after I buy six bolts of blue velvet. The same blood is in my veins as it was back then. What wasn't good enough for you seven years ago still isn't good enough for you. Not that you're interested anyway. But I feel better getting that off my chest. Like I said a while back on the banks of the river . . . we're two adults now. We're not kids anymore. You've chosen a lifestyle and I've chosen a very different one."

"And never the twain shall meet," he muttered.

"That's the size of it," she said.

"I guess that's my cue to leave now, Katy Lynn . . . or is it Katherine here at SD Enterprises?"

"It's Katy Lynn to everyone except Mr. Howard." She straightened her back and kept her chin high. All five-feet-four inches of her wanted to collapse in a puddle at his feet, but Katy Lynn Logan was still as full of spit and vinegar as she'd been when she was six years old. And Joshua Carter would never know how much determination it took to put him in his place.

"Then thank you for the coffee, Katy Lynn, and for being honest with me about your position here. I'll see you in church." He stuck his hand out to shake.

She wasn't prepared for the jolt of electricity that glued her to the carpet or for the way her heart did two double-backward flips. "I'll be there." She was amazed that she didn't stutter or stammer.

He shut the door quietly behind him as he left and she plopped down in her chair. She took several deep breaths. The day had come that she'd prophesied several years before.

I'll show you, Joshua Carter. In five years you'll wish you hadn't been so quick to throw my love away.

It had taken seven years for him to return and he was a preacher, not a worthless rascal, but she sincerely hoped he was wishing he hadn't been so quick to throw her love away.

Chapter Six

Joshua stood before the congregation in his father's church in Nocona. Familiar faces looked up at him in anticipation: his mother, with her graying hair pulled back in a very tight bun at the nape of her neck and topped off with the newest fashion in hats. At least two fancy birds were strolling around naked because that hat had more ostrich feathers on it than one bird owned. Thaddeus sat beside her about to burst the buttons off his new black suit coat. These days his thick gray hair was thinning, his hairline receding and his waist and his jaws getting larger, but there was a look of pride on his face. Joshua opened his Bible and cleared his throat.

"In the beginning . . ." he said and wished that he could have one more beginning. One more with Katy Lynn Logan, who drifted in and out of his thoughts and haunted his dreams every night. But all he'd ever have with her was a slim thread holding together a pastor and a member of his congregation up in Spanish Fort.

After the service he and his parents went to dinner at a restaurant in Nocona. It wasn't nearly as nice as the one everyone frequented in Spanish Fort, but perhaps Joshua had that opinion because it was in that café that he'd seen Katy Lynn several times during the past few months. Nocona was a bigger town than Spanish Fort with a population nearing nine hundred. It had been nothing but a settlement thirty years before when William Broaddus and D. C. Jordan moved fifteen thousand head of cattle into the region and established a ranch in the area. In 1887 surveyors for the Gainesville, Henrietta, and Western Railway arrived and were persuaded by Jordan to extend their rail line across his land. He pledged to donate land for a townsite, and soon thereafter construction of the railroad and the town began. At first the new community was called Jordanville, but then a Texas Ranger suggested the name Nocona in memory of Peta Nocona, a chief of the Comanches and husband of Cynthia Ann Parker. That was about the same time Herman J. Justin moved his boot factory from Spanish Fort to Nocona to take advantage of the shipping facilities. Thaddeus could well remember those days and expounded upon the history of the whole area while they looked over their menus.

Joshua listened with one ear and nodded when he was supposed to, the whole time thinking that he'd never sat across the table from Katy Lynn. Not one time. Back when he was sneaking down to the river to fish a while and kiss a while, he would have been mortified if any of his friends saw him with her. She was the most beautiful girl in Montague County and the one no parent would ever let their son date. That pale skin, jet-black hair, and the hourglass figure with a little more on top than the bottom could balance was enough to take any boy's breath away. Add the crystal-clear blue eyes and she was gorgeous. Lots of fellows had tried to get her to go for a late night ride with them, but she had a wicked tongue that let them know in no uncertain terms she wasn't that kind of girl.

He hadn't even known exactly where she lived. Just that it was somewhere out near the river with her reclusive father. He had gathered up his fishing equipment one night and went to the river hoping to catch a stringer full of catfish. Katy Lynn hadn't even been on his mind and then there she was, sitting on an old patchwork quilt. Her line was already in the water and the routine began. He'd met her there almost every evening and no one knew.

Until somehow Thaddeus found out.

He looked over the top of the menu at his father and remembered the night he ranted and raved and threatened to cut off all prospects of college if he didn't break it off with the girl. What was it he called her that night? Something archaic and strange that only old people would use . . . a hussy? No that wasn't it. A slattern? No, that's what he called Katy's mother. It was a soiled dove.

So that's where she got the name for her roadhouse and business. But how did she know what Thaddeus said? Joshua had been blunt and crude when he broke up with her that horrible, rainy day, but he'd surely hadn't called her a soiled dove. He would have remembered saying those hateful words.

"Roast beef?" his mother's soft southern voice asked and he looked up to find a question in her eyes.

"That's fine," he told the waitress who was looking at him the same way. Evidently she'd asked him what he wanted and he was so deep in thought he didn't even hear her. "I'm sorry. I was wool gathering. Roast beef with mashed potatoes and a tall glass of tea with lemon."

"Wool gathering?" Thaddeus asked.

"Yes," Joshua said.

"I'm glad you consented to preach for me today. The congregation loved having you." Thaddeus changed the subject when he saw the puzzled look on his son's face. Something wasn't right with Joshua since he'd returned to Montague County. Nothing Thaddeus could actually put his finger on, but there was a disturbing quality in his actions. Like sitting there not hearing a word Thaddeus said. Like he was lost in a world of his own.

"Thank you. It was nice to see all those sweet folks. Mr. Howard is delivering the message for me today. He told Katy Lynn to sit up straight and tall, and listen. I never thought about it, but it does help to have people look right at you when you're preaching. It makes the message a lot easier to deliver. A nod of the head and an occasional Amen helps too, doesn't it?"

His father paled. "Who did you say Mr. Howard said that to?"

"Katy Lynn Logan. Remember the girl you insisted I break up with?" Joshua noticed a blush rising to his father's round cheeks.

"Who?" his mother, Ruth, asked.

"You might not remember Katy Lynn, Mother. She was one of those girls from the wrong side of town. Lived down on the banks of the river. I was seeing her that summer before I left."

"I just remember that you fished a lot back in those days. So this Katy Lynn is now a member of your congregation?" Ruth asked.

"Yes, she is." Joshua watched his father's expression turn even uglier.

"That's nice," Ruth said. "Maybe when we come to see you in a couple of weeks you can introduce us. Is she married? You know you need to be thinking about a wife, Joshua. I'm ready for grandchildren."

"No, she's not married." Joshua sipped the tea the waitress put before him. There was a heavy tension hovering between him and Thaddeus. Not totally unlike the night he had gotten into so much trouble. The night he made a decision that affected the rest of his life.

"Well, maybe I can tell her all your good points and play matchmaker." His mother smiled brightly. Katy Lynn . . . his sweet Katy Lynn that he'd called for when he was floating in and out of consciousness when he was burned so badly. So she'd been a Spanish Fort girl after all and not one of his college friends.

Thaddeus spewed coffee all over the table cloth. "You will not," he declared when he could get his bearings. "That girl is nothing but . . ."

"A soiled dove?" Joshua said.

"What has she told you?" Thaddeus demanded.

"Not one thing," Joshua said. "Do you have something to tell me?"

"I most certainly do not," Thaddeus said. "Eat your dinner and let's go home."

Katy sat closer to the front of the church and listened to Mr. Howard deliver the message. He told the congregation that Joshua had gone to Nocona for a few days but he'd be back in his place the next Sunday. Mr. Howard picked up his well-worn Bible and read from the first words in Genesis, "In the beginning . . ."

She wondered if Joshua was courting a lady in Nocona. Had he gone there to get engaged? That might be the best thing. It would bring closure even faster and more complete than an expensive funeral wreath scattered over the muddy waters of the river.

Mr. Howard's opening lines brought back memories of their beginning—Joshua's and hers. She'd taken her rod and reel to the river that evening. Jesse had had a bad day so she couldn't leave him alone very long, but she could fish a couple of hours. Lately, he had had trouble manipulating the crutches and some days he even refused to get out of bed.

It was hot and muggy with a summer shower threatening that never did materialize. She flipped her bobble out into the water and watched the moonbeams dance around it as it sat on the still waters. A thrashing in the woods startled her and she was about to gather her things to go back home when Joshua Carter appeared. She'd been in love with Joshua since he moved to Spanish Fort with his parents. He'd made his brags then that he'd only be living in Spanish Fort a couple of years because preachers didn't stay forever anywhere. But they'd been there six years and she'd been glad he was wrong.

"Hello, Joshua," she said. "Fishing?"

"Yep, what are you doing here?"

"I live back there a ways," she nodded behind her. "Through the trees. There's a path from there to here. I like to fish."

A relationship began that lasted all summer. One that eventually broke her heart and gave her a steely determination to succeed.

"Miss Logan, will you please deliver the benediction?" Mr. Howard stopped her reminiscing cold in its tracks.

She bowed her head and said a brief prayer of dismissal. But they were just words that didn't reach past the ceiling of the church building. What was really in her heart, the thoughts, needs, and wants that only God could discern, could never be formed into words.

"That sorry scroundrel! He's ruining my life, Andy." She plopped down unladylike in a chair at the café.

Andy turned his head to look at her with his good eye. "Who? I'll get the shot gun and we'll make buzzard bait out of anyone upsetting you this much. Is it that Preacher Carter? Did he pay a visit and tell you to stay away from his son again?"

"It's Preacher Carter all right, but not Thaddeus. It's Joshua. I thought I was finished with him, Andy. I thought when he came to the office and I laid it all out on the line for him, when I showed him I hadn't fallen into the little trash heap he expected me to land in, that I'd have some peace."

"But you don't?"

"No, I'm miserable. I'm an old bear. I don't know how Livvy or Marie can stand to work with me. Marie's planning a wedding and I'm not even happy for her because I know I'll have to be in his presence all day," she moaned.

"So what do you intend to do?" Andy asked. "Kiss him or kill him?"

"Neither. He's in Nocona right now. He hinted that he had a lady there. Said he'd been thinking about engagement. I don't want him, but I can't not want him either. One minute I want him to drop down graveyard dead and the next I want to smother his face with kisses."

"Maybe I better shoot him," Andy said.

"Might be the best recourse." She ordered the roast beef with mashed potatoes and extra beans. "I'm starving. How come I always get hungry when I'm nervous or angry?"

"Jesse could eat a whole steer, bellow and horns and hoofs, when he was upset about anything. Guess you come by it honest. I remember once when he had to deliver a speech in front of the whole school, he ate all of his lunch and half of mine. I was afraid he'd be sick on the teacher's shoes." Andy laughed.

Katy Lynn smiled. "Andy, tell me what to do."

"Do? Why it looks to me like you need to get to know this preacher. Next time you see him, look him right in the eye and don't blink and say, 'Preacher Carter, let's me and you take some sandwiches to the river and do a little fishing this afternoon. If we catch something, I'll fry them up for your supper.' I taught you how to fry fish, remember? Lots of cayenne red pepper laced in the cornmeal and hush puppies in the fish grease when you get finished so they'll taste just right."

"He's probably engaged," she said. "And I can't. I promised Thaddeus I'd stay away from him."

"Cost him a pretty penny, too, didn't it?"

She nodded. "You remember that day. He was rude."

"Send the money back to him. With whatever interest it would have accumulated in a savings account for the past seven years. Tell the old lizard you're going to be chasing his son all the way to the Pearly Gates and there ain't one blessed thing he can do about it," Andy said.

She threw back her head and laughed. A real laugh like he hadn't seen in months. Not since the night Joshua Carter had claimed her bar stool and ordered tea, straight up without a drop of anything to cut the sweet. If he'd known that all it would take was good old common teasing to make her laugh like that, he would have said it a lot sooner.

"I might do it." She shoveled a forkful of beans into her mouth. "Is it possible to buy back your word once you give it?"

"Sure, if you're Katy Lynn Logan who owns The Soiled Dove Roadhouse and SD Enterprises, you can buy back your word. Cut him a check Monday morning and send it to him. I'll bet you dollars to donuts he doesn't tear it up and send the pieces back to you in a box."

"I love you Andy." She reached across the table and patted his hand.

"And I've loved you, Katy, since the first day I held you in my arms when you wasn't but a few hours old. Now eat up your dinner. If he's just engaged remember that all is fair in love and war. If he still feels the same way about you that he did that summer when you were sneaking off to the river banks to meet him, the other woman won't have a chance anyway."

"I don't think he does, Andy. I think I'll always be that girl from the wrong side of town who wasn't good enough. But you've made me laugh, and it doesn't look so horrible when we laugh."

Joshua slipped quietly in the door of The Soiled Dove Saloon and found an empty table in the farthest, darkest corner. Katy Lynn's light-blue eyes delivered one message when he shook her hand after church, one of a glimmer of hope. But her mouth delivered an all together different one when she bit his head off any time he went into the general store. He wanted to sit for a while and watch her, see what it was that made someone who owned something as big as SD Enterprises still play a piano in a saloon. She couldn't need the money.

She sat tall and straight and sipped a glass of tea. He could see the wedge of lemon floating in it. She didn't drink. She was a pariah of the town of Spanish Fort, a pillar in his church, and a glorified barmaid. A triple oxymoron. Nothing fit together.

His mother had told him about the weeks he cried out for his sweet Katy Lynn when he was still unconscious after the accident. She thought it was some girl he'd met at school. When she asked his friends none of them knew anyone by that name. He'd swallowed all his pride the previous weekend and told his mother the whole story of that summer when he'd fallen in love with the girl. Ruth shook her wise head and assured him that she'd figure something out by the time they came to visit in two weeks.

A lot of good it would do her to figure anything out. Katy was a beautiful woman. A wealthy, powerful woman who could marry any one of dozens of equally wealthy businessmen. There was no way she'd ever be interested in rekindling an old flame with a scarred preacher man. He watched her look around the room as if she were searching for someone in particular. Maybe she was expecting the man she hinted at being engaged to that day on the river. No doubt he'd be there to walk her home after closing hours. Joshua suddenly needed a drink. Something stronger than tea. He wanted to get smashing drunk and completely pass out. But even that wouldn't take away the dreams. No matter if he got so drunk he was an embarrassment to his whole church or stayed as sober as St. Peter at prayer time, she'd still be there flitting in and out of his mind when he went to sleep.

"Why don't you just ask her to go out to dinner with you?" Ruth had asked him. "Say, 'Katy, I can't seem to get you off my mind. Let's go have a steak.' And I bet she'll go with you."

"I can't believe you'd tell me to go out with a bar-maid." He had laughed.

"A piano player." She'd shaken her finger at him. "Sometimes God works in mysterious ways, my son. We shouldn't judge another person until we've worn their shoes for many miles or many months. People make mistakes. So do preachers. They're just human."

"Thanks, Mom." He had kissed her on the forehead.

It had seemed almost possible when his mother said to just call her and ask her out. Sitting in the shadows of The Soiled Dove brought a reality check. Not only was it impossible. It would never happen. She was too good for Joshua Carter. The realization stripped his soul of all its pride. That was the bare facts. She might be a pi-ano player in a fancy tavern, but he'd heard her praises from Mr. Howard until his ears hurt. Even when he re-minded the elder what she did when she left the store, Mr. Howard just chuckled. "You ever been there when she shuts that place down?"

"Of course not!" Joshua had exclaimed, glad that he didn't have to admit to even being there the one time.

"I was one night. Tried to get her to sell that place or give it to Andy. I've known him for years. Anyway, I thought I was so much better than Katherine and what did a young woman like that need with a saloon? I was wrong, my son. She's a free spirit . . . a wonderful free spirit," Mr. Howard had said in absolute seriousness.

Joshua listened to song after song. He watched people dance, play poker. Money was piled into the middle of the table and swiped away by one and then another. A young man and lady laughed as they pocketed dollars on bets made around the billiard tables. Cowboys bellied right up to the bar and Andy filled their beer glasses. But it was the half-a-dozen women in the saloon that Joshua couldn't believe. Decent women didn't go to places like this. Times had changed and even more changes were in the wind, but it was too fast and too soon.

At five minutes until 2:00, Katy Lynn tapped a fork against her tea glass. The place went silent as a tomb. "Ladies and gentlemen, it's time to shut it down. Go home safely. We'll see you another day."

The poker players stacked the cards in the middle of the table and the billiard players racked the balls and put the cue sticks back on the wall. And the whole house remained deadly silent as Katy Lynn played her own rendition of "Amazing Grace" for the closing number and sang in a clear soprano voice as she played.

The hair on the back of Joshua's arms stood up and a prickly sensation stung the nape of his neck. It was as if he had a vision straight from heaven at that very moment and he knew he was still in love with Katy Lynn Logan. He'd never quit loving her and he had to have her to complete his life.

Katy felt his presence and scolded herself. Joshua wouldn't be in The Dove ever again. It was just a fluke that he'd even stopped by the first time. He was in Nocona with the love of his life—probably with his handsome head on a pillow in his old room that was full of memorabilia from the past seven years of his life, dreaming about his wedding day with the prim and proper Miss So-And-So.

The first night she and Andy had opened the doors, she'd announced the evening was finished and had then played "Amazing Grace" to finish up the night. After that it had become as ritual as her dinners with Andy on Sunday. It was the only church song Jesse liked and the only hymn she'd ever heard her mother sing.

When she finished the song and everyone was filing out of the place she could have sworn she saw Joshua slip out the door ahead of everyone else. But that was just a figment of her yearning imagination . . . and nothing in the world could convince her of anything different.

Chapter Seven

A tall middle-aged woman opened the front door to The Dove and Andy looked up from behind the bar. The lady wore a nice suit and a big hat covered in feathers, most certainly not a person he'd expect to see in the place—she fidgeted nervously as she looked around the dimly lit tavern. Before Andy could ask her if she thought The Soiled Dove was a clothing store or a mission, the back door swung open and Katy Lynn swept into the place.

"Hello," the lady said. "I'm looking for Katy Lynn Logan."

"I'm Katy." Her heels made rat-a-tat-tats as she crossed the shiny hardwood floor. The dark-blue satin of her dress reflected the dim lights and she moved with the grace of a ballerina.

The woman stuck out her hand, "I'm Ruth Carter, Joshua's mother."

Katy's heart skipped a beat, but she shook hands with the woman. Her handshake was firm, her face was warm, and her smile friendly. Katy would have expected anger to be flowing from Ruth's eyes and her mouth to be set in a firm, unsmiling line. After all, the only reason his mother would be standing in front of her was that she'd come to tell her to stay away from Joshua. He and his new marriage didn't need to be threatened by a soiled dove. She might have even been the force behind Thaddeus' anger all those years ago. A strong wife had been the backbone of many men, and perhaps Thaddeus was simply a puppet in her hand. She looked meek and humble and innocent as a new born lamb, but Katy figured she could turn rattlesnake mean any moment. Just like an alley cat. Tame and docile until someone messed around with one of her kittens and then she'd claw your eyes out in a Yankee second. Ruth only had one child and she sure wouldn't want to see him mixed up with Jesse and Mattie Logan's daughter.

"I'm glad to meet you," Katy said.

"I know you're wondering what I'm doing here. I won't stay long. I just wanted to talk to you for a few minutes, and now I don't know where to begin." She laughed nervously.

"Let's sit down," Katy suggested, more for her own benefit than Ruth Carter's. "Did Joshua send you? Andy, could we have a couple glasses of tea?"

"Oh my, mercy, no, Joshua didn't send me." Ruth sat

down and adjusted her hat. "He and Thaddeus are in the church talking about sermons this evening. I'm supposed to be at a quilting bee with some of the ladies. But I sent regrets so I could come here and visit with you. This isn't at all what I thought it would be. It's really a nice place."

"Thank you. Now how can I help you? Thanks Andy. Why don't you sit with us?" Katy looked up at him with pleading eyes when he brought the tea.

"I wanted to talk to you privately," Ruth said.

"Andy can hear whatever we talk about. He's my surrogate father, mother, sister, brother, best friend, business partner, everything rolled into one, and he knows just about everything there is to know about me." She patted the chair beside her.

"Thank you." Andy smiled and sat down.

"Well, a couple of weeks ago Joshua came to visit us in Nocona. Mainly to oversee getting the rest of his possessions moved. But he mentioned you. Just in passing. Something about the deacon who was filling in for him saying that you should sit up and listen. Anyway, when he said Katy Lynn I remembered that he cried for you often before he regained consciousness after his accident," she said.

"Probably just to tell me to never come around," Katy said nervously.

"I don't think so," Ruth said. "Then Thaddeus got all flustered at the dinner table and said you were nothing but . . . and couldn't finish the sentence for some strange reason. And Joshua said 'a soiled dove?' Nothing made a bit of sense to me and I don't like things that aren't put together. You are really quite beautiful, Katy." She changed the subject abruptly and drank a third of her tea while she gathered courage to go on.

"Thank you, ma'am." Katy sipped her tea and wondered just where all this was going and how it was going to end.

"I mulled over the whole thing." Ruth seemed to get back on track. "Joshua and I had a long talk and he said you probably wouldn't go out with him because he's a preacher and he's scarred. The accident, you know. It was very bad and he's got scars that aren't too pleasant. It was a fire and he barely escaped with his life. The house he and some of the other boys lived in caught on fire. Joshua was asleep. Most likely very much asleep, as in passed out from drinking. He was quite the bad boy in those days. But the soiled dove thing just didn't make a bit of sense."

It made perfect sense to Andy and Katy, but they both kept silent.

"So while Thaddeus took his Sunday afternoon nap I made Joshua tell me what he knew. Then when he went for a walk I lit into Thaddeus. It was like prying out hen's teeth, but he finally told me he'd found out about Joshua seeing you that summer. He followed him one night and saw you come running out of the trees and jump into Joshua's arms. He said you were both laughing and kissing. He had a long talk with Joshua and threatened to cut off his financial help if he didn't leave town the next morning without ever seeing you again. I didn't know one bit of this. I just knew that Joshua was so happy that summer and suddenly one night Thaddeus was so angry I thought he'd die of apoplexy, and the next morning Joshua left for school. I thought maybe Thaddeus was regretting letting our son go away and wanted him to stay in Spanish Fort where he could keep an eye on him. I'm digressing again. To make a long story short, I nitpicked until Thaddeus told me about what he did the next day, coming out here after you buried your father and what he said. I'm so ashamed." Ruth blushed.

"That's in the past." Katy patted her hand. "It's over and done with."

"No, it's not," Ruth said. "To think he would act like that is abominable and unforgivable. And him a man of God. I'm mortified at the things he called you. I've come to apologize since he's too stubborn to do so. But I did make him give me something to bring back to you. That's your word that you'd never chase after Joshua."

Katy's breath caught somewhere in her chest and for a minute she thought her lungs would cave in. "Thank you," she said.

"He's not a bad man, but he is a stubborn one who likes to have his own way," Ruth said. "I don't expect you'd be interested in my son. You're a wealthy woman who's beautiful and refined. But he had no right to interfere like that. If he hadn't, you might have at least made an effort when you thought about it—written to Joshua, made up with him, and things could have worked out much differently. I don't believe in meddling in other people's affairs. When we meddle we have to answer for it in one way or the other."

"I don't think it made much difference." Katy shook her head. "Joshua was pretty definite that morning he stopped to tell me it was over."

"I see," Ruth said. "Well, I'll be going now. I just wanted you to know that your word has been returned."

"He bought my word," Katy said. "He paid me money for it and just to get back at him I purchased that piano over there and the sign that hangs above my door which says The Soiled Dove. The only way I'll take the word back is if you allow me to give back the money."

"I didn't know about that," Ruth said.

"Andy will you . . ." Katy started, but Andy was already across the room and opening the hidden safe behind a row of glasses. He removed a large stack of bills and put them into a manila envelope.

"Please give this back to Thaddeus." She handed it to Ruth when Andy laid it on the table.

"He probably won't ever like you," Ruth apologized again.

"I probably won't ever like him," Katy said. "But at least the slate is clean. I've got my word. He's got his money with interest."

"Would you give Joshua a chance if he ever came calling?" Ruth asked.

"I don't honestly know, Ruth. He's a preacher. I own this saloon and I love playing the piano here. Building this kept me sane after my father died and Joshua went away. I don't think a preacher and a soiled dove could ever . . ."

"You better look in that big mirror over there, my child." Ruth pointed to the gilded mirror above the bar. "There are no stains on your wings. Good-bye, now. I hope we meet again."

The ever-blowing Texas wind was brisk that fall morning when Katy stepped up into her buggy. Andy handed her the reins and said he'd see her at the café after the service. She was a few minutes late again and the congregation was singing the first song when she slipped in the back doors. She slid into the back booth beside Livvy, who shared the hymnal with her. Then Thaddeus stepped up behind the podium and Katy's blood ran cold.

"My son preached for me a couple of weeks ago when he was in Nocona and he tells me I have to return the favor this morning. I'm glad to be here . . ."

I bet you are, Katy thought. *But you wouldn't be so glad if you looked all the way to the back of the church and found me sitting here, Preacher Carter.*

Livvy nudged her and laid a piece of paper in the lap of her blue silk dress with a matching jacket. Katy picked up the note and raised an eyebrow. They weren't children anymore and Madge would turn over in her grave if she saw Katy and Livvy passing notes in church.

Are you really over Joshua Carter? He's been here several months and if you aren't going to brand him, then do you mind if I try? He's a good looking man and

I'm asking him to Sunday dinner today if you truly are not interested. Granville and I had a big fight last night and I'm ready for someone new and fresh.

A thousand thoughts ran through Katy's mind. She'd told his mother about preachers and soiled doves. She had her word back so she could ask him to dinner herself, but did she want to? Preacher or not, he might show up on the river banks and tell her it was over after a few months, and she didn't think her heart could stand that again. Could she ever trust him again?

Livvy nudged her again and this time she raised a questioning eyebrow. Katy removed a pencil from her purse and poised it but couldn't make herself write anything.

This is crazy. His mother gives me my word back. His father is preaching in my church. And here I am about to give my best friend my blessings to go after the only man I'll ever love.

She held the pencil for several moments but couldn't make herself write a single word. Instead she just leaned over and whispered, "Go for it," in Livvy's ear and then spent the rest of the service staring at Joshua, who sat behind his father on one of the deacon's benches. He didn't look scarred to her. The dimple in one side of his square jaw deepened when his father told a funny story to bring out a point. She yearned to kiss his mouth when he grinned. And when he raked his fingers through his hair, she wanted to be eighteen again. Carefree. Young. Happy.

It couldn't be recaptured. Not that breathless summer when everything was perfect. Perhaps it would finalize everything if she knew that he and Livvy were together. She'd have to end it or die every morning when she got to work and listened to Livvy brag about the way he could kiss. That idea brought a lump to Katy's throat and she had to fight to keep the tears from her long black eyelashes. She fussed with herself until Thaddeus finished his sermon and asked Mr. Howard to deliver the benediction. Thank goodness, he hadn't looked to the back of the sanctuary and asked her to pray. She couldn't have even remembered "Now I Lay Me Down To Sleep" without stuttering.

"Are you sure?" Livvy's dark eyes flashed excitement when the last amen was said. "I won't ask if you aren't sure. I wouldn't hurt our friendship for any man on this earth."

"I'm sure." Katy shrugged her shoulders.

"Thanks, Katy. I'll let you know on Monday what happened." As usual Katy was the last one in line to shake hands with Joshua that morning. Thaddeus was standing to his left and Livvy greeted him first, flirting blatantly by telling him that she thought he was Joshua's older brother. Surely he wasn't old enough to be his father. Then she took Joshua's hand in hers, batted her long lashes, and said, "Joshua, I thought maybe you and your parents, of course, would like to have dinner with me today."

"That would be very nice, but mother already has dinner prepared at the . . ." he smiled at her, but his eyes were on Katy who was next in line.

"But you'd be welcome to share with us," Thaddeus said. "Ruth makes a mean pork roast and it will be ready by the time we walk across the lawn. You said your name is Livvy?"

"Yes, sir," she said.

"Hello," Thaddeus had Katy's hand in his before he realized who she was.

"Thaddeus," she said softly.

"You haven't changed," he said bluntly, leaving no doubt that he meant she was still a soiled dove in his eyes.

"No, sir, I haven't, but then neither have you," she slipped her hand from his and extended it toward Joshua. She braced herself. Touching her couldn't make his pulse race like it did hers every Sunday morning when they merely shook hands or he would have already asked to be sent somewhere else. If it weren't for losing face in front of Andy, she would have started back to the other church where she was raised . . . where Miz Raven and other women of tainted reputations went. At least that's what she told herself every week. But if she was honest, she knew she wouldn't miss seeing him on Sunday for anything in the world.

"Good morning, Katy." His eyes lit up when he looked down at her. If only it had been Katy who asked him to dinner, but he scarcely thought that his father would have been so generous with his hospitality if it had been.

"Joshua." She nodded.

"Are you having dinner with Andy?" He kept her

hand a bit longer, loving the sensation of merely touching her.

"It's our tradition," she said.

"Tell him hello for me." He finally let go of her hand.

Katy watched from the corner of her eye as he and his mother followed behind Livvy and Thaddeus across the lawn toward the parsonage. She touched her face with the palm of her hand and was surprised that it was cool. It felt like it should have steam rising from it.

"Thought maybe you'd bring the preacher with you today." Andy pushed her glass of tea over to her place like he did every Sunday.

"No, Livvy asked where we stood and she's going to the parsonage to dinner with him," she looked at the back of the room rather than at Andy.

"And how does that make you feel?"

"Empty. But it's better, Andy. If he's with someone else I'll have to let go and go on."

"I think you're wrong. You should give it a try or else you'll go through your whole life wondering if the adult Joshua and Katy Lynn still had the same deep love as the two kids who found it down on the muddy banks of the river that summer. You'll never know if you don't try," he said.

"I can't. A heart can't stand two breaks like that in one lifetime," she whispered.

Katy dressed in a black business suit with a slim skirt, black stockings, and a black silk blouse. She chose an onyx cameo broach from her jewelry box and pinned it on the lapel. She brushed her black hair back away from her face, gathering the thick mass into a chignon net to keep it out of her face. She picked up her purse and slipped on her hat. She looked as if she were attending a funeral and probably was. The death of a love that couldn't survive.

"Well, who died?" Livvy asked when she walked through the door.

"Did someone die?" Katy said.

"Not that I know of," Livvy laughed. "I don't know of anyone who died anyway. But I'll tell you what's alive and well, my friend."

"Is this a surprise or a riddle? You know I hate both of them." Katy hung her jacket on the nearest chair. She expected Livvy to be all smiles and tales about how Joshua did this and that, and how sweet his parents had been to her.

"Neither, I'm going to tell you exactly what I'm talking about," Livvy said. "Joshua Carter is still in love with you, girl. His mother thinks you're a queen and his father thinks you are a two bit hooker."

Katy sat down with a thud. "What are you talking about?"

"Joshua's eyes. I've always shook hands with him when we leave church, but I'd never really stood back and looked at him when he looks at you. It's there. The magic. Someday I want a man to look at me like that. But I'll be hanged if I want one who looks at any other woman with such desire," she said.

"But . . ." Katy started to argue and Livvy put up her palm to stop her.

"But nothing," she said. "It's there. I couldn't brand him if I wanted to. We went over to the house and his mother had dinner about ready. When she found out I'm your friend, she gave me this song and dance about how beautiful you are and what a refined lady you were when she visited with you at the saloon."

"I can fool some of the people some of the time. She actually said in front of Thaddeus that she'd been to The Dove?" Katy managed a weak giggle.

"Yes, she did and she didn't whisper it either. Then I told Thaddeus that we worked together and that you were a very shrewd businesswoman," Livvy said. "He snarled his nose and said a leopard's spots could never be changed."

"Or a dove's wings cleaned," Katy said.

"That's when I laid my napkin down and told him he was an arrogant fool. I told him I didn't care if he was a preacher, he had a lot to learn and I wouldn't sit at anyone's table and listen to him make hateful remarks about my best friend. And I walked out," Livvy said.

"You did what?" Katy's blue eyes were as round as silver dollars.

"I walked out. Joshua ran after me and apologized so I just gave him a piece of my mind while I was good and hot. It wasn't one bit funny then, but it is now. Thaddeus looked like he'd swallowed a live toad frog and Ruth was grinning from ear to ear. And poor old

Joshua didn't know whether to wind his fanny or scratch his watch."

Katy began to giggle like a teenager at the mental picture Livvy drew for her. "Sounds like you sure started a circus with your temper."

"Yes, I did. I just thought maybe if you didn't want him I might like to test the waters. Honey, he's in love with you. And even if he wasn't, I wouldn't do battle every day with old Thaddeus Carter for him. Not even if he owned half of Texas and all of the gold in Fort Knox. That man's an old buzzard."

"You might be wrong about the way he feels." Katy sobered up quickly.

"Nope. He . . . well . . . he . . ." Livvy stammered.

"Spit it out, girl. You haven't have any problem stating your opinion up until now," Katy said.

"No, ma'am. I'm just telling you that much—you have the upper hand. What Joshua said to me out there on the lawn before I left is confidential."

"We've been best friends forever and you're going to take his side!" Katy couldn't believe Livvy.

"Yes, I am. It's because we're best friends. I can tell you what I see and what I feel, but the rest is up to you, Katy. Trust him. Hate him. Brand him. Kiss him. Kill him. It's your ball, your playground, your game. Play it however you want. I just know I don't want Joshua Carter. He's already taken even if neither of you know it yet," Livvy said. "Now we've got Andy arriving in fifteen minutes to discuss the cotton gin in Nocona."

"But . . ." Katy started.

"No, buts, my friend." Livvy hugged her briefly. "I've helped all I can. The rest is up to you. Either you are going to have to think about being a preacher's wife or you're going to have to convert him into a bartender. Those seem to be the two choices you've got."

Chapter Eight

Joshua's attention kept wandering from the children who were reading passages and hanging the green Christmas wreaths around the sanctuary. Katy Lynn was in charge of playing the piano for the whole program. The children ranged from the youngest Sunday school class members as they presented their part of the program to the oldest teenagers singing songs as they climbed ladders to place greenery between stained glass windows.

It was a beautiful ceremony, one he had participated in from the time he had been a small boy until the last time when he was sixteen and read the scriptures. But right then he was having a bit of trouble listening to the young, blond-haired teenage boy who read with such lovely expression. Joshua had trouble controlling his restless thoughts because he couldn't keep his eyes off

Katy Lynn, who was playing the church piano for the first time since he'd arrived at the church.

The elderly lady who played on Sunday morning had told him just that morning that Katy always played for the Christmas program. "My Sunday school class sings 'Silent Night', and I'm in charge of most of the program, so about five years ago I talked Katy into playing. She has been taking care of the responsibility ever since then."

Katy Lynn arrived fifteen minutes before the beginning to warm up, and she bustled past him without even seeing him in the throng of kids needing last minute attention. But Joshua most certainly saw her. She wore a red velvet dress with a high neckline and long fitted sleeves. It fell in a swooping skirt all the way to her ankles. Matching velvet shoes peeked out from the hemline and her hat was just a pouf of lace on top of a frill of matching velvet. Angels straight from heaven couldn't have been more beautiful in Joshua's eyes.

In church she played the piano with the same passion that she had at The Dove all the nights he had slipped in the back door and listened. He'd always chosen a chair in the back corner beside the door so he could escape right after she played "Amazing Grace." He'd been going there more than one night a week for six weeks and he had thought she would realize he was sitting not fifty feet from her, but she hadn't.

The ache in his heart was worse in the church. Just looking at her across the room, his palms were clammy and his mouth felt like it had been swabbed out with a cotton ball. If she walked up to him and asked a question, he would have stuttered and stammered like a thirteen-year-old school boy.

He'd played the "if only" game too often and lost every time. He gave himself an ultimatum after the fiasco with Livvy a few weeks before. If Katy didn't give a single sign that she was still interested by the New Year, he fully well intended to find someone to seriously date. He might never know that breathless excitement he had when he was with Katy Lynn, but perhaps preachers shouldn't have that in their lives.

She tilted her head to one side and played "Silent Night," so softly it made him sigh with desire right there on the front pew of the church. The five- and six-year-old children were singing in high squeaky voices, sincere in their efforts and as off key and out of tune as Katy was in tune and on key. If there was one miracle floating around up above the rafters of the church, Joshua wished it would fall on his shoulders and she would give him something more than a passing comment with a handshake on Sunday morning.

"This has been a beautiful service," he said at the close of the ceremonies. "We'd like to thank Katy Lynn Logan for playing for us tonight and also to the church ladies who have refreshments in the fellowship hall. Everyone is invited to join us for an hour of fellowship and food."

Katy Lynn poured punch and Livvy served cookies to the children and their parents as they filed past the refreshment table. Marie's mother had decorated a small cedar tree for the centerpiece and the candles put a soft blush on her cheeks.

"Lovely job." Joshua's fingertips brushed hers when he took the crystal punch cup from her hand and that old familiar tingle started at the nape of his neck and crept up to the top of his head. Even if he married another woman, he'd never forget the way he felt when he made physical contact with Katy.

"Thank you." She smiled. "Weren't they cute when they sang 'Silent Night'?"

"Yes, they surely were." He smiled back. Was her smile the miracle he'd prayed for? Or at that extra sentence? She usually just answered his questions quite bluntly. He couldn't remember her actually initiating a conversation. She'd spoken her mind and even stepped up on a band wagon, but never with a sweet smile.

"Joshua." Mr. Howard tugged at his arm. "We've got a lady who wants to meet you personally. She's visiting a daughter and she's leaving tomorrow to go back to Arkansas . . ."

The miracle was over.

An hour later, Katy Lynn and Livvy had finished cleaning up and were the last ones out of the fellowship hall.

"Oh, I can't leave. I almost forgot." Katy Lynn started down the hallway with Livvy at her heels. "I left my music on the piano in the sanctuary. I'll go back and get it. You go on. I'll see you at work on Monday."

Livvy waved. "It should be a big day. Holidays.

People still have shopping to do. And we've got to think about the final touches on Marie's wedding, so don't be late."

"I'll be there." Katy Lynn opened the door to the dark sanctuary and made her way to the front of the church. She fumbled around on the piano top until she found the last music she'd played. The rest of what she'd brought along was on the bench in a neat stack where she'd left it.

"Hello." Joshua startled her when he spoke from the front pew.

"Joshua?" She almost reached out to grab her heart and shove it back into her chest.

"I came back for a few minutes to quiet down." He told a half-truth. What he'd actually come back inside the sanctuary for was to pray earnestly for help in dealing with the attraction, both physical and emotional, he had for a woman with no use for him.

"Well, I forgot my music."

Walking past him was almost impossible, but she managed to make her weak knees go right on as if he weren't there. Every fiber in her body screamed for her to sit down beside him and tell him exactly how she felt. That she loved the sensation when his fingers touched hers at the punch bowl. That she really wanted to talk a little more about the children and how cute they were when they rolled their eyes toward heaven as they sang. But he'd come to the sanctuary to quiet his soul or whatever preachers did when they needed to draw near unto the Almighty. He certainly hadn't come for an old flame to plop down beside him and confess her hidden feelings.

A few drops of rain had begun to fall when she eased the front door shut and her heels made a tapping noise across the concrete sidewalk. Rain, even though nothing more than a mist to block out the stars, brought back a flood of memories. The latest ones slowly replacing those on the creek banks: Joshua's smile when he shook hands with her. But then he smiled at everyone, she chastised herself. She inhaled deeply and it was there. That woodsy aroma he'd worn since he first started to shave. She used to shut her eyes when he walked past her on the school ground just so she could capture the essence. Rain and Joshua's cologne. It was a hell of a thing to have to take home to a lonely bed.

She reached for her umbrella in the back of the buggy only to find it gone. She'd been in such a hurry to get to the church to practice a few minutes before the program that she'd left it in the stand beside the front door. She should have known better. The clouds had threatened rain all day, but there was the matter of gathering up all the sheet music and she hadn't been able to keep her mind on anything but Joshua since Livvy had gone to dinner with him and his parents.

That only left one alternative. Did God strike people dead if they disturbed a preacher's meditation time? Well, if He did, He'd better get the lightning bolts lined up because she wasn't going to ruin her brand-new dress by driving home in the rain.

"Katy?" Joshua called from the church steps.

"I forgot my umbrella. I need to wait it out in the church," she raised her voice just slightly.

"You can come home with me so I can change clothes and then I'll drive you home in my closed buggy." He drew his suit coat around his chest tightly and motioned for her to follow him. His prayers had been answered. Maybe not in the way he'd wanted. But it was a beginning. Half an hour in a buggy was something. That's more than he'd had so far.

He was just a few feet from her when she said, "I can wait in the church until you come back."

The skies opened up in a sudden downpour. He reached out his hand, took hers in his, and she did what came naturally. She ran along beside him as the cold rain blew in from the north and literally soaked both of them to the skin.

"Whew." He shivered as he opened the parsonage door and held it for her. "Hurry or we'll both freeze to death."

She hustled into a small but cozy living room. She didn't know where to stand. Her velvet dress dripped on the floor, making puddles that looked like blood, and her shoes were a muddy mess. "I'm ruining your floor."

"Don't worry. Follow me. You will catch pneumonia in those wet clothes." He took her by the hand again and pulled her down the hallway. "Get out of them in the bedroom." He opened a door and lit a lamp. "I'll hand you one of my robes. It will swallow you, but at least it will be warm. There are towels under the wash stand. Get dry. That will help take the chill off."

"Thank you," she whispered.

"I'm afraid your dress is ruined," he said.

"Probably." She let go of his hand and shut the door. She moaned when she saw her reflection in the mirror. Dark, limp, and wet hair stringing down her back and in her face. High color in her cheeks . . . like a school girl out on her first date.

She stripped out of the dress, corset, corset cover, slip, and underpants and stood naked before the vanity, drying herself vigorously to bring warmth back into her skin. When she finished a soft moan escaped from the depths of her soul. Her hair would have to come down so it could dry, and a woman did not let her hair down in a man's presence unless he was her husband.

"Katy?" He knocked on the door and she opened it just enough to reach a hand out for the robe. "Could I make you a cup of hot chocolate or coffee to take the chill off before I take you home?"

"Coffee. Black as sin and twice as strong." She didn't care if she offended him with her language.

He chuckled and she heard his bare feet padding down the hallway. The deep dark-green flannel robe came to her ankles. She rolled up the sleeves and wrapped the sides completely around her body, belting it into her small waistline and looked like an orphan or maybe a half-drowned raccoon when she stepped out of his bathroom.

"I'm following my nose," she called down the hall as she made her way to the kitchen. "I smell coffee and I hope it's as strong as it smells. Andy says if it doesn't hold up a silver spoon in the middle then it's nothing but murdered water."

His heart soared. The miracle hadn't escaped him after all.

"Momma says if it don't stain the inside of the cup you've wasted your time making it." He met her in the middle of the living room. "Green looks good on you Katy Lynn."

"I look like something the dogs dragged home and the cats wouldn't have. But I'm grateful because it's warm and it covers me up. I can drive myself home, Joshua. As soon as this lets up. I should have brought the covered carriage. You don't have to get out in this messy weather and take me home."

"I don't mind. Besides what would people think of their pastor if he didn't lend a helping hand to his biggest supporter?"

She just smiled, a real one that reached all the way to her eyes and made them sparkle. It was the first time Joshua had seen highlights in her eyes since he'd returned, but he hoped it wouldn't be the last time. She shivered, but it wasn't from the cold on the outside. It was the first chilly wave leaving her heart as it began to warm toward Joshua Carter in spite of the fact that her better judgment knew to not trust him.

"Coffee should be ready. I've got the remainder of a chocolate cake if you'd like something . . ."

"Just coffee. I ate more of those little cookies than I could count," she admitted as she pulled out a chair and carefully wrapped the robe around her body before she sat down. There was nothing else between her body and his eyes. Streaks of jagged lightning shot through the windows, threatening to strike her graveyard dead if she let the preacher see even one inch of shin bone.

He carried two cups of coffee to the table. It was evident he'd just towel dried his hair in hurry—dark strands spiked every which way and the part was nonexistent. At least he didn't have to worry about looking like he was thirteen, like Katy did. Faded denim jeans hugged his rear end and muscular thighs well enough to make Katy just about swoon right there in the parsonage living room. The dark green shirt made the highlights in his brown eyes even more pronounced. Would God overlook just one hug?

"So why did you forget your umbrella? It's been threatening rain all day." he exclaimed.

"I was in a hurry." She sipped the coffee. Just right. Black as tar, strong as sin, and hot enough to burn the hair off a frog's tongue. "I was in a hurry, thinking about getting to the church early to practice my music, and walked off without it. Didn't even realize I didn't have it until I grabbed for it and it was gone. Not that it would have helped a lot the way this rain is blowing."

"You said you have a covered buggy?"

"I've got two, yes. A covered one and an open one. Andy thought I should bring the covered one, too, but I told him I wanted to breathe the fresh air. When this stops and you take me home, I'll get Livvy to help me drive my open one home tomorrow after work. Oh, dear, I forgot about the horse."

"I'll hitch up my horse behind the buggy when this stops and then ride back home," he offered.

"That should cause the gossip vine to go into flames. You with me looking like this," she said.

"Then I'll put your horse down in the church stable and you can bring someone tomorrow to help you get your rig home. I'm sure he'll be fine until you get here."

"You've done enough."

We'll see, he thought but didn't press the issue.

"What made you go into business? When we talked about our future you were going to be a school teacher," he said.

"I found out what teacher's earn," she laughed, her voice a mixture of pure clover honey and red hot blazes that made him want to listen to her all night long. "I made more than that each month from my share of the general store. You remember I was working there when you left? Then it came up for sale and Livvy inherited a small house from her grandmother and Marie had a few acres of land she'd inherited from an uncle. So Andy helped us and we bought the general store. I had this idea for the saloon because Daddy always said he'd wanted one but it wasn't a fitting place to raise a daughter. He had some savings I didn't know about so Andy and I had it built. Then we had a few dollars to invest and a hotel was for sale. After that we bought a couple of floundering businesses and turned them around. Made a good profit. Bought a few more. Couple of years later we were doing very well."

"I see," he said.

"What about you Joshua? You were going to do anything but preach if I remember right." She could probably tell him word for word what he said most of those hot summer nights.

"I wasn't a good student when I left here. You are right. I wasn't going to go anywhere near a church or a preacher. I squandered away a whole year, had a really bad accident and then went back to school. I'm content with my choices, Katy Lynn." He longed to reach across the table and take her small hands in his. "If you're finished, I'll take you home. Give me time to hitch up the horse and get your rig into the stable. I'll bring mine around to the front door."

"I'm ready. I'll gather up my things. Would you have a box or bag to put them in? I'll be sure to return your robe in a few days, as soon as it's laundered."

"Sure." He found a small wooden crate in the kitchen and handed it to her, careful this time not to touch her hand at all.

Half an hour later he opened the front door and motioned for her. He helped her into the buggy just as the sky opened up again with a violent crash of thunder and more bolts of lightning. Rain was still pouring in great sheets and Katy drew the robe tighter around her body as she hugged the far side of the buggy.

He drove slowly. Rain. He always remembered Katy Lynn when it rained. The way she stood there so proud when he told her she was from the wrong side of the town and he couldn't ever make a life with her. It had just begun to rain that day and it rained all the way to

Nocona. The night the house burned down it rained after the place was too far gone for the firemen to put the blazes out. The only thing he really remembered about the fire was waking up in pain with her face in his memory. He'd thought then if only she would touch him he wouldn't hurt anymore.

He took a deep breath and the sweet smell of a cold winter rain mixed with her perfume filled his mind with visions so real he could almost touch them.

"Katy, would you go to dinner with me one day next week?" he asked quickly.

"I don't know, Joshua," she said honestly. "I've been on the verge of asking you the same question after church every week. I know women aren't supposed to ask men to go stepping out with them, but since you are my preacher, I suppose it wouldn't be a great sin to ask you to Sunday dinner, especially if Andy was there. There's enough of a physical love left over from when we were kids for me to want to see you. But there's enough common sense to know that we don't . . . that we can't ever build on . . ."

"What?" he asked when she stopped and stared at the wind and rain.

"Joshua, I was in love with you when I was in pigtails and you came to town. It never went away, so there's an attraction there, but I've grown up now and so have you. I'm a business woman, but I'm also half owner of The Dove. A glorified saloon. You are a preacher. There can be no better future for us as adults than there was when we were kids. I was from the wrong side of the town then and I still am. I told you that. The blood in my veins still hasn't changed. My parents aren't saints just because they're dead. So I don't know how to answer your question."

"That's a heck of a thing to say." He slapped the seat between them.

"That's pretty close to cursing. You might not value your life out here in all this thunder and lightning, Joshua Carter, but don't bring the wrath of God down on my head because you can't control your wicked tongue. I'm just being honest."

"You're just throwing it back in my face." His temper flared so hot she could feel the heat. "You're just getting even for the time I was ugly. I just want to get to know you, Katy Lynn Logan, to see if there is something left to build on, before I go on . . ."

"On to what?" She raised her voice right back at him.

"Nothing. Not a blasted thing," he swore again.

"Joshua Carter, you better watch your mouth or I'm getting out and walking the rest of the way home. My luck would be better in the rain than with a swearing preacher."

"You'll do no such thing," he said. "I'll take you home. Right up to the door. Which reminds me, do you have a house key or is it back there with your buggy, also?"

"I keep one hid under porch step," she said.

"Under the porch step. Katy, that's crazy! You live alone. Everyone puts a house key under the porch step. Anyone could come in and hurt you." He hadn't lost his temper in years. Not since before the fire. After he awoke from his comatose state he'd made a vow to God and he'd kept it . . . until this black-haired vixen straight from hell had provoked him to cursing.

"Don't you tell me what's crazy or not, Joshua," she huffed. "At least you won't have to put up with me all night. I'm going home and you can have your peace and quiet back. You could have just let me drive home in the rain. I was already wet anyway."

"Oh, hush," he snapped.

"Don't you tell me what to do," she fired right back at him as he stopped at the side of her house. With the roof over the pathway from the house to the back door of The Dove, it was impossible to drive up to her front door. "The time when I might have listened to you has long since passed. Thank you, Joshua for bringing me home." She all but growled out the thanks.

"You didn't answer me," he said when she bailed out of the buggy and got ready to run from the truck to the front porch. "Will you go to dinner with me?"

"Persistent, ain't you?" She set her full, gorgeous mouth in a firm line. "Yes, Joshua Carter, I will go to dinner with you. But let me tell you right now, up front, I'm not that backward girl who you used to know. I'll tell you exactly what I think and if you don't like it, you can go . . ."

A bolt of lightning crashed through the sky and danced around the trees. "Be careful," he grinned. "Thank you for saying you will go. When can I pick you up?"

"Not until after the wedding next week. I'm too busy and have too many irons in the fire until then. Call me after Marie is married and we'll talk about it then." She wanted to seal the promise with a kiss. Even a chaste one on his cheek, but instead she ran to the house. She fished out her spare house key from under the porch and waved to him after she opened the door.

Joshua slapped the reins against the horse's flanks. Drat the woman anyway. She could have just simply said she would go with him when he asked the first time. She didn't have to make a big issue out of it. A simple yes would have saved all that arguing and fighting.

Katy pulled the curtain back and peeked out the slit until she couldn't see the buggy anymore, not even by the lightning. She'd provoked him to anger, but he'd made her mad enough to chew up railroad spikes and spit out ten penny nails. She inhaled deeply . . . his cologne with just a touch of rain water. She wondered how long the scent would last and how long she could keep the robe before she had to return it.

Chapter Nine

The wedding dress hung from a hook in the ceiling of Katy's living room. It was richly trimmed with embroidery, had a yoke inlaid with lace and a lace collar, long sleeves embellished with embroidery, and a belt of Venice lace trimmed with satin rosettes. The extra-full skirt extended to a wide flounce with two rows of tucks around the bottom. Livvy, Marie, and Katy had spent days pouring over catalogs and magazines coming up with the design that Miz Raven had finally created. The veil of illusion and pearls was draped over a rocking chair and the box with the satin shoes inside was sitting on the settee.

"Okay, girl, it's time to get this on," Katy called down the hall to Marie, who was having one more piece of chocolate pie to quiet her nerves. "We've got thirty minutes until the ceremony and you're not about to be late for your own wedding."

"You should see Davy." Livvy pushed the front door open. "He's just the most handsome man in the saloon in that black suit and his hair all slicked back. He's as nervous as a long-tailed cat in a room full of rocking chairs. I swear, he's going to pace all the wax off your floors out there."

"Wow, wait 'til Joshua sees you." Marie whistled through her teeth at Katy Lynn when she got to the bedroom.

"That's enough." Katy waggled a finger in her direction. "This is your day."

Katy and Livvy were identical in forest-green satin bridesmaid's gowns, cut similar to the wedding gown with high collars and long, full skirts. Except, at almost six feet tall, Livvy felt somewhat like a giant when she stood beside Katy.

"Okay, I'm ready for help," Marie said when she'd donned her corset, white eyelet-lace corset cover and underpants. "Did I really pick that thing out? Or did you two talk me into it?" She looked up at the dress.

"Us?" Katy widened her eyes in mock shock. "Would we do something like that?"

"Yes, you would." Marie held her arms up for them to drape the dress over her head and fasten all the satin buttons up the back and on the sleeves. "Too bad neither of you can wear it. We could get triple use out of the thing."

"Oh, no," Livvy said. "I'm eloping. Somewhere exotic and I'm wearing one of those new bathing outfits. I'm thinking maybe we'll take a trip to an island where women don't have to wear so many clothes."

"And when is this going to happen?" Katy asked.

"Probably sometime next summer. I met my groom last week, but he doesn't know he's a groom yet so don't tell him. He might even come to the wedding. I invited him. He's six-feet-two-inches tall and he fills out the hind end of his britches just right. Gives me the hives just thinking about how well," she blushed.

"Good grief, Livvy. Nice women don't talk like that. Who is this man?"

"He came into the store while you two went to get us some lunch. That day when everything was hectic. He said he was in the area looking about buying a ranch and trying to get to know people. He just about took my breath away. His name is James Dalton and he asked me if he might have a glass of tea with me this afternoon at the café, so I just invited him to the wedding."

"Oh my, and this dress will be way too short for you." Marie got a case of nerves and had trouble standing still. "But we could shorten it for you, Katy."

"Not me," she laughed. "I'm the old maid. I'll spoil whatever kids you two have and play the piano for The Dove until I'm so blind they have to lead me out there and put my fingers on the keys. I'll have wispy gray hair and . . . be still or we'll never get you buttoned up in this thing," she scolded. "I'm glad you're leaving in your wedding dress and we don't have to undo all this.

Poor old Davy may get so frustrated he won't remember what he's supposed to do when he gets all the buttons undone."

Marie giggled. "I'll put a thousand-dollar wager down that you beat Livvy to the courthouse for a marriage license."

"You're on," Katy said. "I haven't even met a tall, lanky rancher who has a nice hind end and gives me the hives."

"I want in on it too," Livvy said. "I'll dance a jig in a pig trough at my own wedding if I get married before you do, and honey, I'm dragging James to the altar just as soon as I can catch him."

"What is this? Gang up on Katy Logan day?"

"Nope, just stating facts," Marie said. "Now let me look in the mirror. Oh, is it really me? I'm almost pretty."

"You're absolutely gorgeous." Katy hugged her gently. "Let's get the veil on and help you get into those shoes. I told you to walk in them an hour every night so they wouldn't pinch your feet."

"I was afraid I'd get them dirty. Besides I can kick them off after the ceremony. The dress will cover my bare feet and I'll already be married, so it won't be a disgrace."

Katy walked down the two rows of chairs from the back door. The whole place was draped in yards and yards of white illusion and lace, caught up systematically in red velvet bows. The mirror behind the bar reflected the light from hurricane lamps, spreading a soft glow to the room. Katy was glad to see that even though it was a holiday and a Sunday afternoon, every seat was filled. She carried a bouquet of white poinsettias in a bed of feathery fern and winked at Davy as she took her place at the piano. Nothing doing but she'd be a bridesmaid and walk in as such, but she had to play the piano so her duties were split. Her hands landed naturally on the keys and she began to play.

She'd carefully avoided looking at Joshua standing so tall in his black suit. She watched Livvy make her entrance at the back door and sweep elegantly down the aisle toward the front of the road house. Then the doorway was filled with Marie, on her father's arm and everyone stood up.

Katy meant to sneak a peek at Davy, to see what his first reaction to Marie was, but her glance got sidetracked when she found Joshua staring at her with such intensity, it took her breath away. A smile tickled the corners of his sensuous mouth and his eyes glittered. Then he winked, ever so softly and slyly. Just a wink between two people who'd been in love and still couldn't shake the feeling.

"Dearly beloved," he began the ceremony when Marie reached her place. "We are gathered here this glorious winter day to unite this couple in holy matrimony . . ."

Katy listened, but she didn't hear a word. Just the intonation of his voice as he blessed the union with a prayer made her heart race. Was she serious when she told the girls she would be an old maid?

Probably so. Because I can not have Joshua. That's a

given. We can go out to dinner. There can even be a love to surpass all eternity, but there can never be a union with a preacher saying a prayer for us. I never was right for him and that hasn't changed.

After the ceremony, Katy sat on her bar stool and nibbled on piece of white bride's cake with sugar icing. Joshua mixed and mingled with the people and seemed to be ignoring her completely. Evidently he had realized what a mismatched couple they really were and had decided not to even ask her out to dinner. Perhaps he wouldn't stay in Spanish Fort very long and he'd simply go away and she'd learn to deal with it again. Only this time, she'd just have a bruised heart, not a broken one.

"Katy, you've got to meet James," Livvy said at her elbow.

"Well, hello." Katy's eyes kept traveling upward until she reached the blond curls of a tall man who truly did look like he'd been put upon the earth just to stand beside Livvy.

There ain't no way I'll beat Livvy to the courthouse. Lord, that man looks like he's been thunderstruck.

"I'm glad to meet you. Livvy just told us today about you." Katy extended her hand.

"Katy?" Joshua was suddenly beside her.

"This is James," Livvy said. "And I'm stealing him away to dance with me. Marie and Davy already did the first dance and we've had cake. Since it's a wedding maybe we'll be forgiven for dancing on Sunday? Do you think?"

"I don't think. I know. I came to ask for a dance," Joshua looked at Katy.

"Baptist preachers do not dance."

"This one does," he said. "You are a very beautiful woman today, Katy," he whispered as he drew her close for a slow waltz playing from the Victrola. "I like that as well as any of the costumes you wear to play the piano."

"Oh? And how many costumes have you seen me in?" She leaned back to study his face. "Just a red sequined one if I remember correctly."

He just chuckled. "And a blue velvet, and a green satin, and a bright blue silky think with black lace trim."

Suddenly she knew why she'd felt his presence in the roadhouse. He'd been there lots of times, sitting in the back shadows where she couldn't see him. "So why didn't you step right up and say hello?"

"School boy rejection syndrome. If I stepped right up, I'd have had to let you know how I felt and you might have told me where to go."

"I still might."

"I wouldn't doubt it." He pulled her close again, glad to be able to hold her so close he could hear the beating of her heart keeping time with his.

"Why did you buy such a fancy piano?"

"It seemed fitting."

"How's that? Was your father partial to piano music?"

"He and my mother both. They like the bawdy songs from a saloon. He said Momma's voice singing along with the piano player is what drew him to her in the first place. That and the color of my mother's eyes. He loved her blue eyes. And of course, he had an attitude and a Knight In Shining Armor thing. She was the bad girl and he would give her a name and a home and she'd be like Cinderella. It didn't work, but he liked blue, anyway," she said.

"Then why didn't you have the piano painted blue?"

"Hey." Livvy tapped on a glass. "Marie is about to throw the bouquet, so all unmarried women need to line up behind me. I intend to fight to the finish for it." She laughed.

Katy stood behind Livvy, along with a dozen other young women and Marie turned her back. She tossed the bouquet over her left shoulder and Livvy stepped aside just as it flew in her direction. It floated right into Katy's arms.

"You traitor. I stood behind you because I figured there was no way I'd ever catch it."

"I don't want to dance a jig in a pig trough at my wedding." Livvy patted her on the shoulder. "Now, let's go throw rice at the couple and let them get on to the honeymoon."

Marie and Davy drove off in a fancy carriage decorated with old boots and cans thumping along behind them in the traditional fashion. Joshua stood close enough to Katy that she could feel the heat from his body as well as his gaze. It must be wedding fever. Lots of guys got it when they saw a bride all fluffed out in white lace. Suddenly they had visions of a perfect little wife, cooking perfect little meals in an immaculate little house where pansies and petunias grew in the window boxes.

Well, that might have happened in Thaddeus and Ruth's house, but it sure didn't happen in the house where she grew up so he could just blink away that blissful look in his eyes and take a headache powder for the wedding fever.

"The wedding is over. When are we going out to dinner? Mother and Dad are arriving tonight for Christmas tomorrow. Want to make it Tuesday night?"

"How long are they staying?"

"Until Wednesday morning."

"I wouldn't take you away from their visit on Tuesday then." She asked herself if that was really the reason or if she didn't want to think about what Thaddeus was going to do when he heard that his son was actually going to be seen in public with the soiled dove he hated so badly.

"Wednesday night?" He followed her back into the saloon. People were busy putting the place back into order. Livvy had James and four other men helping undo the illusion from the walls, but the hurricane lamps still filled the place with a warm glow.

She sat down at the piano and tickled the keys. There had been no actual dates between Katy Lynn and Joshua, just lots and lots of nights on the banks of the river. So Wednesday would be the day, and his deacons would meet him on Thursday and tell him he'd just made the social blunder of a lifetime.

"Aren't you busy at the church on Wednesday night?"

"Not this one. We canceled all services because of

the holidays," he reminded her. "You never did answer me about the piano."

"I ordered it special," she told him. "Black like my heart felt that day when you left and your dad came right up in my yard to tell me to stay away from you. Thaddeus paid for it and the sign out front."

"What?" He cocked his head to one side, unable to believe what she'd just said.

Surely he knew. His mother had said they had a long talk and she brought her work back to give to her. She had to have told him about Thaddeus. "Oh, Joshua, you know. Your mother said you two had a long talk."

"When did you talk to my mother?"

The cat was out of the bag and she had no option but to let it howl. "Your mother came to see me right here last month after you'd gone to Nocona and said that you two had a long talk. Livvy said when she had dinner with you that Ruth mentioned she'd talked to me. She brought my word back to me, and I just figured she had told you."

"Maybe you'd better tell me right now. Mother said she'd visited with you, but I figured it was in the general store, not here." His voice had a cutting edge to it that she didn't like. His eyes flashed prideful anger and his jaw muscles left no doubt that he was nearing the boiling point.

"Okay, I'll tell you about it. Your father came to the house after you left that morning. Remember you said we were finished. It was over. Just a fun summer that in five years we would forget. I was going to amount to nothing. I think that's pretty close to what you thought, anyway," she said curtly. "You were gone. I'd just buried my father and here comes Thaddeus with his attitude sticking out a mile in front of him."

"What did he want?"

"He said I was to never to chase after you or have any contact with you. He had an envelope with money in it and he laid it on the porch railing. Said he wanted my word and he'd buy it. I told him he didn't have to pay for it. He could have it without money. But then he got hateful and called me a soiled dove. So I picked up the envelope and used the money to buy this piano and that sign out there. Do you have a problem with that?"

"Yes, I do," he stood up abruptly. "You didn't love me enough to fight for me."

"You didn't love me enough to fight for me either, Joshua Carter. All he had to do was threaten to cut off your finances and you ended it with me. Remember, I was the girl from the wrong side of the town or river or whatever it was." She stood up and took a step into his space, her nose just inches from his.

"You didn't need the money and you took it?"

"Yes, I did take it and no, I didn't need it. I even knew I didn't when he put it up there. The day before I only knew I had a job at the general store. I didn't know I'd buy the store in a few days. I didn't know it, but Daddy had this money he'd saved when he was on the cattle trails. Money that he and Andy kept investing and reinvesting. It was a lot. What's it matter anyway? You were off drinking your life away and making deals with

God." She didn't blink but stared right into his gorgeous angry eyes.

"Don't you blaspheme just because you're mad at me." He raised his voice.

"Don't you yell at me, and I wasn't mad until you got on a high horse about the money. I figured your mother told you about it when she had her little heart to heart with you. Or at least told you that she'd brought my word back to me. She said Thaddeus was too stubborn to bring it himself."

Joshua turned his back and walked away from her. She was so tender when she was waltzing with him in the middle of the dance floor. So wonderfully sweet when he winked and she'd blushed scarlet. And so aggravating when she argued with him. Well, he didn't need that kind of aggravation in his life. If she couldn't be sweet one hundred percent of the time, then he could slam the doors of her glorified saloon and get on with his life. Which did not include one Katy Lynn Logan. Good lord, what on the great green earth had ever made him think for a minute he could recapture that crazy summer? History did not repeat itself in every instance. She'd sold out for a piano and a sign that mocked his father's wisdom. Well, she could sit at her piano until she was old and wrinkled and that sign could swing in the wind and rain until the hinges rusted and it finally came tumbling down.

Katy didn't know whether to laugh or cry. Tears seemed like such a waste on a total idiot, even if he was a preacher. She'd already cried enough to flood the river in the middle of July for Joshua Carter and it hadn't changed his pompous attitude one bit. He was so full of himself it oozed out of the pores and dripped on to the floor before him as he walked. It was an amazement that he didn't slip and fall in his own ego juices as he tried to get out of the abominable saloon.

She stomped her foot and picked up the bridal bouquet she'd caught just minutes before. He wasn't going to walk out on her again. Not without a fight. She drew back her right arm and chunked the bouquet as hard as she could. It hit him in the middle of the back just as he opened the door and he jerked around.

"Don't you dare . . ." she screamed across the room full of people.

"Dare what?" he yelled right back.

"Ask me to dinner and then act like the south end of a northbound donkey," she gritted her teeth.

"Me? What are you acting like?"

"I will be ready at seven o'clock sharp on Wednesday night. We're going to have dinner at the café right in the middle of town where everyone and his dog can see us. Afterward I want to sit on the banks of the river so they can see you bringing me home alone without a chaperone. You'd better bring a coat. And I don't have to explain jack squat to you, Joshua Carter, about why I'm acting like this."

"I will pick you up at seven, Katy Lynn," he said through clenched teeth. She wasn't ever going to be able to say that he didn't keep his word.

"I'll be ready." She sat back down at the piano and

started playing "Amazing Grace." It was over now. Time to shut down the house and go home.

The beautiful wedding with all its sentimentality was over. She and Joshua were finished. Their love had died in the middle of a tirade over a big black piano. The bouquet she had caught had been transformed from an omen of good will into a funeral wreath. Now all they had to do was go to dinner on Wednesday night and bury the whole thing.

Chapter Ten

The first snow flakes of the year fell silently on Katy's black hair when Joshua opened the buggy door for her. This was their first real date and the tension was so thick they needed machetes to hack through it. He was formally polite, attentive to every detail, a total stranger who had haunted her dreams and caused her to awake in a cold sweat night after night. She was colder than the bitter north wind whipping her long skirt tail around her legs. A beautiful ice queen with a heart he could never touch again . . . maybe never even had in the beginning.

"Still want to go to the café?" he asked.

"That's fine. Just make it very public so people can see that you are having dinner with me." She kept her eyes straight ahead and didn't even look at him.

He felt rather than heard her inhale deeply when

they reached town. "We can go anywhere you like, you know. There's more than one place to eat in town," he said.

"The café is fine. I guess I thought it would be different. If you had taken me on a real date back when we were eighteen this is where you would have taken me."

"I don't think this town will ever change very much," he said, ignoring the barb.

She stepped inside and let him pull out a chair for her.

Joshua was right, some things never changed and he was probably at the top of the list.

She slipped out of her long coat and draped it over the back of the chair. A bright-blue waist stretched across her more than ample bosom and picked up the color in her eyes, but there was no pink excitement in her cheeks. She folded her hands in her lap and waited. Joshua knew where she stood, so he would start the stilted conversation.

"My folks left yesterday morning," he said. "Mother was elated that we were having dinner tonight and Dad was ready to bite bullets."

"Like you said, some things never change."

"I'm twenty-six years old as of yesterday. I value my father's opinion on lots of things, but you're not one of them."

"Happy birthday." She looked up into his eyes and wished desperately that things could be different. "I don't guess we ever got around to talking about birthdays, did we?"

"No, when is yours?"

"I'll be twenty-six on March 15. Beware of the Ides and all that," she said.

"Good Lord, is that really you Katy Lynn Logan?" A chubby fellow with two chins and a receding hair line stopped beside their booth.

"Hello, Matthew." She smiled brightly and a surge of pure green jealousy went through Joshua. "I haven't seen you in years."

"Not since the night I left town to work on the railroad. I'm just riding through on my way to a family reunion over the weekend in Burlington. So what did you become when you grew up?" He pulled a chair from beside one of the tables and sat down with them.

"I still work at the general store," she said. "And I built a saloon out by the river."

Matthew chuckled. "Maybe I'll stop by on my way back home. When are you open?"

"Every night but Sunday," she answered. "You would remember Joshua Carter? He went to school with us."

"No, can't say as I do, but then I was only here for that one year," Matthew said. "What kind of business did you get into, Joshua? I'm an engineer for the railroad."

"I pastor a church here in Spanish Fort," Joshua said. "I think I remember you. Weren't you the kid who liked to play marbles?"

"That's me," Matthew nodded. "Well, I'll catch you another time. Maybe I'll stop by the saloon and take a look."

"I'll look forward to seeing you," Katy said.

Matthew shook hands with Joshua and disappeared out into the blowing snow.

"Mmmmm." She made appreciative noises as she bit into hot, greasy fried potatoes. "I love good food. Maybe some day I'll even learn to cook." She bent forward and sniffed the aroma of a pork chop done to perfection.

"Do you often see old classmates?" he asked.

"Sometimes they drop in the saloon. When it first opened a bunch of your cronies came in, but they didn't stay long. They were looking for a joint where they could start a brawl. They were pretty abusive when I told them to leave. Andy stepped in and it didn't take them long to get out."

"Katy, I never told a single person about that summer," he said.

"Oh? Well, I went out and told the whole town. I even put it in the newspaper. "Katy Lynn Logan Kisses Preacher's Son" was the headline. I even let them use a picture of the two of us with big fish between us. Remember that one?"

"No, Katy, we never had a photograph taken of us. Believe me, I would remember that."

She had to smile in spite of everything. "Tell me, Joshua, just why are we here?"

"To have dinner and then we're going to the banks of the river in a snowstorm. We're going to sit there like we did one night long ago. But I'm not going to put my feet in the water when the snow is flying around out there," he answered.

"A person can't go back," she said. She'd just driven that point home by coming out in public with Joshua. The world had kept right on turning and she'd bet dollars to donuts that the sun came up the next morning right on time.

"Nope, but they can sure go forward and not look back," he said, looking into her blue eyes and seeing a touch of warmth. He yearned to reach across the table and take her hand in his, to brazenly pull her to her feet and close to his chest to dance like they did in the saloon after the wedding. It didn't matter that there wasn't a bit of music playing in the café. He could still hear the music being played at the wedding and he could hum it.

"Are we really going to go down to the river on a night like this?" she asked.

"Chicken?" he taunted.

"Not on your life. If you can do it, I can do it twice as fast." She threw out the challenge.

"Then finish your dinner, darlin'. And we'll just see who's freezing first," he said, grinning.

She tried to capture the image of his smile in her soul so that any time she wanted she could shut her eyes and see it again and again.

He caught her stare and held it as long as he could.

The snow had picked up slightly and big flakes drifted down from gray skies as they drove back to her house and walked down the path to the river's edge. Water flowed slowly just like it had done for years and years. The ghosts of lots and lots of romances roamed both sides of the banks, she was sure. She drew her coat closer, shoved her gloved hands down deep into her pockets, sat down in the cold dirt. That summer it seldom ever rained. Most nights, the stars twinkled making a bed for a big old lover's moon. She and Joshua swam in the moonlight, playing underwater chase, finally lying on their backs, with an audience of squirrels who from a pecan tree chattered at them for disturbing their world.

"Hasn't changed much," he said, sitting down beside her. Six inches separated them, but it might as well have been six miles.

"No, it hasn't." she leaned back and caught a snowflake on her tongue. "We don't get snow every year, you know."

"I remember," he said. "We got it often in Virginia."

"I'm ready to go home now." She stood up abruptly. "I'll make you a cup of coffee to chase the chill away."

"Okay," he said, following her lead back up the path to her small house.

Over and done with, she told herself as they warmed their hands by the embers in the fireplace. If someone wrote it up for the newspaper, they could say that the funeral had been held at the local café, internment was on the banks of river, and the family supper was a cup of coffee following the services at the home of Katy Lynn Logan. There were no survivors—only a soiled dove and a preacher left to mourn.

"Coffee sounds good." He followed her across to the kitchen. She tossed her coat on the back of the sofa and he did the same, taking in the whole room in a single glance. A big stone fireplace on one end. Floor to ceiling bookcases on either side. A dining room, kitchen, and living room all flowing together without the benefit of doors.

"Daddy had trouble getting around with doors so he had the house built for his convenience." She went to the kitchen and filled a pot with water. "I'm making hot chocolate. Do you mind?"

"No, not at all." Actually, he was elated she was making chocolate since it took a little longer than coffee. "I like your house, Katy. It's got a lot of personality."

"Thank you. I probably should sell it and build something else, but it's hard to leave home. This is all I ever knew. Would you throw a couple more logs on the fire? I've got fruit cake left from Christmas if you want . . ."

"No, just chocolate. What did you do for Christmas?"

"Andy and I made dinner like we always do. Chicken because we couldn't ever eat a whole turkey. Dressing, cranberry salad, pecan pies, fruit cake, all the rest of the trimmings. Then we sit in front of the fire place and open presents. Isn't that what all families do?" She kneeled in front of a grate of logs and lit a couple of pine cones with a long match.

"Pretty much." A peace surrounded him that he'd never known before and he didn't want to leave. He and Katy could just shut the doors to what everyone thought, to the whole world, and live in a cocoon of contentment.

"Marie's mother always makes me a big bag of fire starters," she said, holding up a pine cone embedded in wax with a wick on one side. "They are wonderful and work like a charm. Andy says her husband better watch out or he'll steal her away from him."

Joshua laughed. "Chocolate smells good."

"Yes, it does." She looked up into his dark eyes.

His face moved closer and closer until his mouth found hers. His lips were still chilled and tasted like fried potatoes. It was delightful. She teased his upper lip with her tongue and wanted the kiss to go on forever.

He wrapped his arms around her and drew her close to his chest without breaking away from the kiss. Her lips were beginning to warm and he'd never known that simple fried potatoes could leave such a wonderful taste behind.

"Joshua," she mumbled.

"Mmmm," he mumbled. He tightened the embrace and the final fetters fell from her heart and her willpower flew out the window into the soft snow.

"I missed you so badly." He buried his face in her hair, inhaling the mixture of shampoo, snow, and what was just naturally Katy Lynn.

"Me, too. I missed you," she said.

"Katy, there's something I need to . . ." He let the sentence hang as he removed his collar and unbuttoned his shirt.

"What are you doing?" she gasped.

"I'm not the same man I was when I left here. There was a fire. I was drunk out of my head and passed out cold. If the firemen hadn't carried me out, I'd be dead. For several months I wished I was. My shirt had burned and stuck to my back." He removed the shirt and turned around. "You need to see this before we go any further."

Her heart hurt for him. His back was a mass of puckered burn scars and his voice barely a whisper when he said the last sentence. She reached out and ran her fingertips down the rough scars. "I'm so sorry." She took a step closer and laid her face against his bare back, brushing kiss after kiss over the scars as if they were children again and her kisses could heal them.

"They don't repulse you?" His voice caught hoarsely.

"Nothing about you could ever repulse me, Joshua," she said.

They had no need for words past that point. He put his shirt back on and they stretched out with mugs of hot chocolate, their backs against the couch. After a while they set the empty mugs aside and laced their fingers together. That was enough for the night: enough of a foundation to begin to build something better.

He awoke with a start and checked the mantle clock: 4:00. The sun would be up in a couple of hours and he really should wake her. But she was sleeping soundly and a niggling fear of rejection still hung on in his heart. He couldn't bear the idea of her waking up to tell him it was over and not to ever come back again. He eased away, grabbed a quilt from the back of the rocking chair, and gently covered her up.

He found a piece of stationary on the kitchen table where she'd been making a list. He tore off a sheet and wrote, *You are so beautiful when you are asleep. We need to talk about what we're going to do about us. You were sleeping so soundly, I couldn't wake you. Please come to the parsonage today. Love, Joshua.*

He laid it on the pillow beside her face and picked up one sock, looked around for the other one and finally just shoved his bare feet into his boots. He grabbed his coat and shut the front door ever so gently to keep from waking her.

There was definitely hope after all.

Katy was dreaming about rain and thunder and lightning. She awoke with a jerk, throwing her hand up toward her face to keep the flash of lightning from her eyes. The breeze from her hand sent Joshua's note flying under the edge of the sofa. For a moment she wondered what she was doing on the living room floor. Then she grinned and turned in one fluid motion to cuddle up in Joshua's arms. She'd wake him slowly with kisses and then make him a working man's breakfast. Only there was no Joshua. The only thing left of him was a lingering aroma of his cologne and precious memories of a wonderful evening.

He'd left her again. And she'd been fool enough to think he'd still be holding her in the crook of his arm, her head on his shoulder when she awoke. Like she'd said, "You can't go back." Why hadn't she listened to her own advice?

Bright sunlight streamed in the window, but no warmth came with it when she realized she was alone before a bed of cold ashes. He could have at least awakened her and kissed her good-bye. But it was pretty darned evident he'd had second thoughts sometime after she went to sleep in his arms. He was there. He was gone. History sure enough did repeat itself.

She shivered and wrapped herself in the throw. The smell of chocolate still permeated the whole kitchen area. She poured the last drops of something resembling black tar down the sink. Then she checked the table, the counter, the credenza just inside the door.

Nothing. Not a note. Nothing to tell her why he left without waking her.

It could only mean one thing. Well, Joshua Carter wasn't coming back to Katy's house again, not ever. Or to her heart either.

One of his socks peeked out from under the sofa and she absently mindedly bent down to pick it up. Tears flowed down her cheeks as she hugged it to her chest but she resolutely carried it to the trash can and tossed it inside. If only she could toss her heart in with it. Just get rid of the hurting lump of pain in her chest. But she couldn't, so she'd have to get on with life.

She prepared a bath. Even hot water couldn't erase the tingling in her body when her mind kept replaying the soft kisses from the night before. It would never happen again. Not only would it never happen again, could never happen again. Katy Lynn couldn't bear to see him walk away time and time again.

Chapter Eleven

Joshua wasn't in The Soiled Dove on Thursday night. She deliberately checked every corner when she took her break. Besides the feeling wasn't there like it had been the past several weeks. That crazy catch in her heart or the faint whiff of his cologne wafting across the glasses of beer; neither was there.

Friday night she appeared in her electric blue costume with black lace trim and didn't even bother to check the dark corners. He wasn't coming back. He'd checked the waters, found them too hot for his preacher's blood, and was holed up in his little house hoping that she had dropped dead before Sunday morning.

On Saturday night she decorated the roadhouse with silver-and-gold crepe paper streamers and got everything ready for a New Year's Eve party. She didn't open the joint on Sunday and since that was officially New

Year's Eve she'd told everyone they would celebrate on Saturday. By 10:00 the house was packed and noisy, but Joshua wasn't anywhere in the crowds.

"Well, hellllo." Matthew sidled up to the piano where she was playing. "Who woulda thought old shy Katy Lynn Logan would be sitting in a place like this, dressed up and playing the piano like she was born with her fingers on the keys?"

"Who'd a thought it?" She smiled up at him and didn't miss a single note.

"What happened to the preacher man? He too good to come in here?" Matthew sat down beside her on the seat and deliberately let his shoulder touch hers.

There was no jolt of desire. Not even a faint little glimmer of a spark. Just a pudgy fellow in loose fitting trousers, a new white shirt, and a bead of sweat on his upper lip. "Joshua has church tomorrow morning," she said.

"Am I moving in on his territory?" He slipped his arm around her waist.

Someone yelled, "Ten . . . nine . . ."

She looked at the clock, the second hand clicking off the time until midnight.

". . . eight . . . seven . . . six . . ."

Where was Joshua? He should be riding a white horse through the doors to carry her off to live happily ever after. *How crazy,* she thought and stopped playing as she watched the clock, mesmerized. He should have been there to kiss her at the stroke of midnight.

". . . five . . . four . . . three . . . two . . ."

"Happy New Year," Matthew shouted in her ear as he

wrapped both arms around her and planted a kiss firmly on her mouth. He gritted and ground until her mouth felt more like it had been molested than kissed passionately.

"Maybe that will wipe the preacher out of your mind," he said, grinning when he released her. "What do you say we check out of here for the rest of the night and go finish up the night in my room at the hotel in town?"

"No, thank you. I'm playing until two when we shut the doors." She shook her head. "Besides I'm not that kind, Matthew."

"Oh, sure." He ran a finger up her arm to her bare shoulder. "Don't tell old Matthew that. Someone runs a joint like this and dresses up like you do. Honey, you are hot to trot. I know women like the back of my hand."

"The answer is still no." She picked up his hand and dropped it like a piece of trash. "Happy New Year. Now I think it's time for you to leave."

"I'm going." He snorted when he laughed. "I'm in room ten if you change your mind and want a good time later on. If you're not there by three I'll let in the other five women I've already invited to the party."

"Have a good time." She frowned and picked up her tea glass. She held it up to Andy and nodded toward Matthew.

"Trouble?" Andy asked when she reached the bar.

"Could be. I want him out of here. If he's not to the door in five minutes then get rid of him," she said.

"Looks like you've already done it. He's picking up

his coat from the back of a chair and headed toward the door. I saw him kiss you and wondered if you might need some help. Lord, girl, why'd you even talk to the likes of that slimy character?" Andy asked.

"I didn't. He ran into me and Joshua last Wednesday. We were in school together back when we were little kids. I didn't know he was going to come in here or kiss me. Fill up my tea glass please and put lots of lemon in so I can get the taste out of my mouth." She snarled her nose.

At 2:00 she played "Auld Lang Syne" instead of "Amazing Grace," and the customers filed out still singing about old acquaintances and kissing each other under the mistletoe hung above the door for good luck. She began to set the chairs upside down on the tables while Andy pumped water into the mop bucket.

"I think we broke the record for profit tonight," he said, rolling up his sleeves. "What happened when you and Joshua went out, Katy? You've acted like you lost your best friend all weekend. And he hasn't even been sneaking in the back door like he usually does. Just sits in the back booth. Watches you play and then high tails it out as soon as you play 'Amazing Grace.' "

"You knew about that and didn't tell me?" she snapped.

"Sure. Figured if he wanted you to know he'd tell you. And if you still loved him, you'd figure out he was in the place." Andy squeezed the soapy water from the mop.

"It's over for good this time, Andy, and I don't want to talk about it," she said. "I'm tired. What do you say we take a couple of days off. We aren't going to be open tomorrow night, so let's skip church on Sunday, sleep until noon, and make dinner at my place for the real New Year's. For New Year's Eve we can stay up late and tell stories about Daddy when the two of you were young. Like we did when I was a little girl."

"Sounds like a winner to me. Let's make fried chicken for supper tomorrow night and you can make the gravy," he agreed. "But this is the only Sunday or Joshua will be thinking that whatever happened, he's run you out of the church. And Katy Lynn Logan," he leaned on the mop, "you are a stronger woman than that."

"Yes, sir," she saluted smartly. "The gravy will have lumps."

"You need the practice or you'll never find a husband." He laughed, down deep, a real man's laugh.

"Then it will always have lumps." She snorted.

When Joshua reached the parsonage that morning after spending most of the night with Katy Lynn, there was a strange man sitting on his porch. "Son, your father has took a spell. Your momma sent me to bring you to Nocona. We would've sent a telegram, but with the time, she thought it best if I came on. I got here about an hour ago and been waiting for you. She said the doctor said it's an emergency and not to waste time."

He packed a suitcase, stopped by Mr. Howard's at the unholy hour of 5:00 in the morning and told him he needed him to take over while he was gone, and was on his way to Nocona. Then he remembered Katy. But surely Mr. Howard would tell her what had happened the next time he was in the store.

By Saturday Thaddeus was better but still unable to get out of bed. The doctor said he'd had a near heart attack and needed rest to recuperate. Joshua delivered the New Year's message in Nocona and Mr. Howard preached to a sparse congregation at the church in Spanish Fort. Twice a day, Joshua walked to the telegraph office hoping for word from Katy, but there was nothing. Every day he checked the post office for a letter. His pride kept him from sending a message to her.

By New Year's Day, he'd lost all hope. She'd just been toying with his emotions, getting back at him for walking out on her. Someone once said that paybacks were hell. They didn't know the half of it. If she went through as much pain in the days after he left as he was going through while he waited for word from her, it's a wonder she hadn't dived into a pool of alcohol just like her mother had done all those years ago.

Surely it wasn't the scarring on his back that had sent her running away from him, he thought as he sat beside his father's bed after four days. If it turned her stomach the way he feared it might, she wouldn't have laid her face on it and kissed it. No, it was simply that she was getting even with him, and whether he liked it or not, he deserved even worse.

"Son, did you really go out with that Logan girl last week?" Thaddeus grunted as he tried to sit up.

"I did." Joshua nodded.

"Did you realize that she's not your type after all?" Thaddeus asked.

"I did not, but I think she realizes I'm not good enough for her," Joshua said.

"You what?" Thaddeus sputtered and moaned.

"I'm not good enough for her, Dad. Do you know what I did? I broke her heart. We had all these plans and there she was burying her father and I just coldly rode up and told her that it was over. I said we'd look back in five years and realize it was just a summer of fun," Joshua said.

"She was just a . . ." Thaddeus snarled his nose in disgust.

"A soiled dove," Joshua finished for him. "No, Dad, she wasn't. We were so much in love it was awful, but Katy Lynn didn't want to be like her mother. She said she was holding out for our wedding night. That we'd never be sorry. You know what her sin was, Dad? She had been in love with me for six years. That's a sin to love someone as cold hearted as me for six years. I'm going to bed now. I'll be going back home tomorrow. Mother said one of your colleagues has agreed to step in and help out next week."

"You got things all wrong," Thaddeus argued.

"No, I've got things all right," Joshua shook his head. "I just wish I'd had enough wisdom back when I was eighteen to realize I was killing the dove. The one you see is a soiled one . . . but she's the same dove, Dad . . . only the one I see is a peace dove because she brings peace to my life and tranquility to my soul. And neither one of us is ever going to know what a contribution she might have brought to our family."

Thank God for that, Thaddeus thought but was in too much pain to say.

Livvy stumbled into SD Enterprises on Tuesday morning. "You two better go first and tell me about your holiday since I've got a case of love fever," she declared, holding her palm on her head.

"That means you didn't make it to church on Sunday." Katy tested the waters with a nonchalant voice and held her breath.

"Guess you didn't either or you wouldn't be asking," Livvy said. "Lord, no, I didn't make it to church. James and I decided Friday night that we were going to go down to Nocona. We checked into a hotel. Don't look at me like that. We had separate rooms. I plan to marry him, not seduce him. We spent the whole weekend looking for land for him to buy."

"Have a good time?" Marie popped around the corner carrying a tray with three cups of coffee.

"Yes, ma'am. I'm going to marry that man so you two can just get ready to start planning a wedding. So how'd the honeymoon go?" she asked Marie.

"Absolutely beautiful," she sighed. "I didn't want to come home and I sure didn't want to crawl my hiney out of that big feather bed and come to work this morning. Davy says for me to sell out to you two and be a ranch wife. He's got all those acres and cows, and he declares we're already rich as Midas. I think he wanted me to be there when he came in for dinner today," she said wistfully.

"Well, James bought a couple of miles of land down around Prairie View and I'm just about ready to join you in your boat," Livvy said. "Soon as he proposes I may be a rancher's wife."

"How about you, Katy?" Marie said. "Wasn't Joshua pressing you to go out to dinner with him?"

"Yes, he was, but it didn't work out," she told them. "Now, I don't want to hear another word about selling out. SD couldn't run without you two and you know it. I've got to go back to Gainesville this afternoon and finalize that deal. I'll be gone until Thursday morning. There's not a lot going on, but if a gold mine comes up for sale for a dollar ninety-eight while I'm gone, you two hop right on it. Livvy, take a couple of aspirin and put a cold cloth on your head. There's a cot in the back room. Take a nap. We'll manage the store this morning. I won't let anyone open the door but James." She took charge to keep from thinking about Joshua again.

"You are a sweetheart," Livvy moaned and started off toward her office.

"You won't think so when you are dancing a jig in a pig trough in a few months." Katy giggled. "Marie, I do need to get the paperwork ready. I'm packed and Andy is going with me. We've shut up The Dove for the next few days. Business will be slow or nonexistent anyway."

"I know. No one is to disturb you. Not even Joshua?"

"Especially not Joshua. Not that he'd come around anyway. I told you we found out we are not compatible."

Joshua walked the floor at the parsonage. Mr. Howard came by early that morning for a catch-up on what was going on. Joshua forgot what they'd talked about and paced some more. He went to the ice box and took out a pumpkin pie his mother sent home with him. He cut a quarter of the pie, topped it with a little cinnamon, and shoveled a chunk in his mouth. It had absolutely no taste.

He scraped the rest into the trash can and slapped the counter top. If Katy wasn't going to come by and tell him what had happened, then he'd go have it out with her. At least a rousting good fight would get him out of the lethargic state he'd fallen into. It might not accomplish one blessed thing but a screaming match, but at least they'd get their problem aired out.

He put on his coat and hat and headed out toward the general store. The events of the night played through his mind as he walked, oblivious to the cold. He had kissed her on the forehead and put the note right beside her face. It had to be the first thing she saw when she opened her eyes and she ignored him. At least he'd had the decency before he left to tell her it was the end.

He walked past the café and his resolve began to wan. Did he really want to confront her right then? Perhaps he should go inside and have a cup of coffee and take the edge off his anger before he went charging into the general store. He pushed the door open, went inside, ordered coffee, took two sips, and realized nothing was going to cool down the heat but confronting Katy Lynn and having it out with her. He had to stand in line to pay the cashier since it was almost dinner time and the rush had already begun. A part of him had hoped that perhaps Katy would be in the café having an early lunch. Surely in public they could have settled their differences without a war erupting. But she hadn't been there, so evidently God didn't care if there was a war.

He slung open the general store door at a quarter after twelve. He hoped she didn't have a luncheon date with a client, and that she would at least see him. They might raise the roof in her fancy office before they got all the dirty laundry on the line, but before quitting time that afternoon, Joshua fully well intended to get it settled with her. One way or the other he was going to have some peace. He might be an old bachelor, gray or balding, bent in his back and shuffling along with only memories of a dark-haired, blue-eyed beauty who had broken his heart. Or they might find a common ground, go on with their relationship, and wind up together through eternity. Either one would be better than the vacuum he was floating in right then.

He bypassed groceries, fabric and sewing notions, cookware, and the check out counter and slung open the office door to find Marie sitting at the desk, her nose in a stack of files and a bowl of popcorn in front of her.

"Hello," he said. "Is Katy in?"

"No, she's out for the day," Marie said without looking up.

"Joshua." Livvy peeked around the corner. "What are you doing here?"

"I wanted to see Katy." His face showed absolute misery and disappointment.

"She won't be back until the end of the week. She had to go away to work on a deal we are thinking about getting into. I might remember the name of her hotel if I think hard enough," Livvy said.

Marie shot her a dirty look. "She said she didn't want to be disturbed."

"Oh, she did, didn't she?" Livvy put her hand on her forehead. "I had a bit of a headache. I guess I'm still fuzzy headed. See you in church next Sunday. Sorry I missed last week."

"So did I." Joshua wanted to kick something. The trash can. The desk. Even the glass out of the fancy door behind him would do just fine. "My father took ill and I was gone over the weekend."

"I'm sorry," Livvy said. "Got to get back to work."

"Thank you for your time," Joshua said curtly as he backed out of the office. "I'll be back in the pulpit on Sunday. Maybe I'll see Katy then."

"I'm sure you will. She didn't make it Sunday because of the party on Saturday night, but you wouldn't know about that since you weren't there," Livvy talked in circles, making very little sense.

Joshua went straight to the river. He sat down in the cold dirt and picked up a handful of dry clods. He rubbed them together in his big hands and let them sift through his fingers as he tried to make sense of his world. It had seemed so orderly before he moved to Spanish Fort. He'd made his decision and never looked back, but right then as the cold sand drifted through his fingers he wondered if he would ever find happiness again.

Katy checked into the hotel in the middle of Gainesville. She'd tried to sort through the confusion on the train but every thought hit a dead end. She finally decided she would confront him when she got home. She was going to have her say-so even if it caused him to start swearing again.

She opened the drapes on the fifth floor of the hotel and watched the snow filter down past the street lights below her. Everything was already white and she'd heard one man say on the train that they might shut down the railroad the next day, but she wasn't leaving until Thursday so she wouldn't worry about it until then.

She paced the floor and wished she could talk to him right then. She tried to think about the deal they were about to make, about what she'd wear to supper that evening at the restaurant just off the hotel lobby, but all she could see was Joshua baring his back for her to see. Trusting her with his shame. She threw herself across the bed and finally slept away part of the afternoon. But it wasn't a peaceful sleep. She dreamed about Joshua and Thaddeus standing outside the general store and screaming for the soiled dove to come out so they could burn her at the stake.

Chapter Twelve

Joshua drove to the saloon on Thursday night and sat on the porch swing in spite of freezing weather. He tilted his Stetson hat down over his eyes, drew his overcoat tight against his chest, and shoved his hands in his pockets. He could hear the sweet strains of piano music drifting in and out the door as people came and went, but he couldn't make himself go inside.

On Friday night he forced himself to stay in the house and read. Pure self will and determination made him finish the book by 2:00 Saturday morning, but when he completed the last page he didn't even know what he'd read. She'd called the shots when she told her friends and coworkers she didn't want to be disturbed. However, if by Sunday night she hadn't called on him, he fully well intended to ring her doorbell and have it out with the vixen. Under the stars and to the top of their lungs if necessary.

Katy Lynn played the piano that Thursday night, but her heart wasn't in it. Not even when she finished up the evening with the familiar old hymn. It was as if Joshua was on the fringes of her mind constantly. He wasn't in the saloon or she would have felt that tingly, prickly heat in the pit of her soul. Yet, his presence was almost there. By the time she'd tossed and turned the rest of that night, worked all day Friday, and then played the piano again on Friday night, she was so angry she could have battled a forest fire with a single cup of water. She wouldn't confront him on Saturday. That wouldn't be fair at all since it was probably the day he was getting his message ready for Sunday morning. But if he hadn't made some kind of overture after ten days then he was going to get a royal raging piece of her mind.

She was ten minutes early to church on Sunday morning and sat in the middle of the church on a pew all alone. She wanted him to look out over the congregation and see her that morning. To see the woman who he'd spurned for the second time.

"It's good to be back," he said when he stepped up behind the podium. "I want to thank Mr. Howard for delivering the message last week. My father is recuperating well from his illness and Mother says he's starting to get cantankerous so I suppose he really is getting better." He smiled when everyone chuckled, and that's when his brown eyes locked with Katy Lynn's blue eyes. "My message this morning is from the fifteenth chapter of Corinthians." There was no one in the whole church from that moment on as he preached to himself and looked at her. "It's the love chapter and it says in plain English that love is not unkind, does not want its own way . . ."

Right, she thought, *don't you ever practice what you preach, Joshua Carter. You were the unkindest man I've ever known. You've broken my heart. Not once but twice, and just when did this illness thing happen with Thaddeus anyway?*

When the service ended he asked an elderly man sitting in the pew right in front of Katy to deliver the benediction, and he tiptoed down the center aisle to the back of the church to wait to greet the people. She bowed her head but couldn't keep her thoughts on the final Sunday prayer. In a few minutes she would shake his hand and he'd greet her in a cold business manner as if they hadn't even shared that night of sweetness.

He managed to get through the pleasantries. She'd always waited to be the very last person so he was surprised to look up and see her in the middle of the string of people coming out of the church. It had started to sleet so folks were either bypassing him altogether or else barely speaking as they dashed out to their rigs. Finally she was standing before him with her hand out and a cold glitter in her blue eyes.

"Katy?" he said.

"Joshua?"

"I would like a few minutes with you," he said.

"Oh, that's a surprise. In private or public?" she snapped.

"Could you meet me in my office in ten minutes?" he asked just as snappishly.

"No, I can not," she said. "Andy and I have a dinner engagement. If you've got something to say to me, Joshua Carter, you can call me at home this afternoon. I'm planning a long nap so anytime after four will be fine."

"I see." He had trouble controlling the anger boiling up from the tips of his shiny well-polished shoes. "Well, then I will get in touch with you after four. Have a good lunch and give Andy my regards. Hello, Mrs. Smith." He dropped her hand and reached for a middle-aged woman next in line. "And how is your grandson? Did he get over the chicken pox?"

Her palm burned from his touch in spite of the bitter cold sleet beating down on her head and leaving her hair in limp strings. So Joshua Carter wanted to talk, did he? Well, so did she and he'd better clean off a place inside the parsonage or the church because she intended to have a first class hissy fit. She'd have lunch with Andy and then come back for the fight of the century. There was no way she could take a nap with all that on her mind.

Andy pushed a cup of steaming hot coffee across the table toward her when she hurried into the restaurant for lunch. "Thought that might suit you a little better on a nasty day like this. Was Joshua there today? Heard his father had a bit of sickness and he wasn't in the pulpit last week."

"When did you hear that?" she questioned.

"This morning while I waited on you. That waitress over there with the big ears told me. Her mother goes to the church and she said Joshua Carter had to go to Nocona in a hurry. Guess it was an emergency or something. Anyway she says she thinks the preacher is good looking and she'd even quit her swearing for a chance at him. I don't know. Them big ears would have to go, don't you think?" he teased.

"I don't care if he gets a hooker from a brothel," she snorted. "Lord, it's so cold the chill is all the way to my bones, Andy."

"Methinks me hears a bit of jealousy in your voice," he said.

"What you hear is pure mean mad," she said, leaning across the table. "And as soon as I get some sustenance in my stomach I'm going right back up to that church for a fight. If you see flames over in that direction you'll know I've shot the sorry rascal."

"Careful, you're talkin' about one of God's chosen," he said, shaking a finger at her. "And I'm sittin' too close to you for comfort if the lightning starts. I'm thinking I'm hearing the first strains of wedding bells?"

"Then you have something terribly wrong in your head, Andy. I'm going for a fight not a proposal." She dived into the salad the waitress set before her with the gusto of a hungry hound pup. "We're going to bury this thing today and next week I'm going out with the first man who walks through the doors of SD Enterprises without a wedding ring on his finger."

"What if it's that creep who kissed you at the New Year's Eve party?" He raised an eyebrow over his black patch.

"Yuck," she said with a shiver.

"I think you better rephrase that statement to attacking the first man who looks presentable." He accented each word with a jab of his fork. "I'd hate to think I had to walk you down the aisle toward the likes of that fool."

"If he was the last man on earth and I was the last woman the race would die," she shivered. "Andy I'm so mad I could spit."

"Well, eat your dinner first," he said. "And then go have it out with Joshua."

"But what if it's really over. I mean final and finished and there's no more chances?" she asked.

"You'll know at least and you can quit hankering for what can't be. Fight with him. Love on him. Tame him. Shoot him or whatever. Just get that lost look out of your eyes and let's get on with life," he said.

"Okay." She nodded, but suddenly she wasn't so sure she was really ready to face him down.

Joshua turned down two invitations to lunch and ate a cold ham sandwich with mustard and lots of pickles. It had absolutely no flavor, but he forced himself to eat every bite. He watched the sleet for an hour and then decided he wasn't waiting until 4:00 to have it out with Katy. She'd called all the shots up until that moment, but it was time the tide turned.

He put on his coat and headed out to the stable to saddle up his horse when he saw her stomping up the street. He waited. She shuddered with every blast of sleet but it looked to him like she'd already built up a steamy head of anger. He almost felt sorry for her. She should be home cuddled up in front of a blazing fire with a good book and a soft pillow, not out braving the weather just to talk to him. But the sympathy didn't last long, not when he remembered how she'd ignored his love note.

"Katy?" He opened the door. "Shall we go inside?"

"No, this is just fine," she said, shaking her head. "How could you walk out on me twice? The first time you were young and your father was on a warpath. But I thought things were going to be all right when we snuggled up together in front of the fire."

"Hey, wait a minute." He held up a hand. "I didn't forsake you last week. That was your doing and there's no way you're going to blame me for that one. Right, I was young, easily influenced and not very smart at eighteen, but darn it if you're blaming me for last week, Katy Lynn Logan."

"Almost swearing on Sunday?" She raised an eyebrow.

"Even God would understand." He shook his head in dismay. "The Almighty Himself would have trouble keeping his tongue around you."

"Well, thank you so much," she snapped. "I don't see where you're coming from telling me this whole fiasco is my fault."

"I awoke at four o'clock that morning." He glared at

her. "You were sleeping so soundly I hated to wake you so I slipped out of the house . . ."

"That's a likely story after the fact now isn't it? Eleven days, Joshua, and not a single word," she whispered.

"I did not forsake you. I did put the ball in your playground and I thought you'd at least get in touch with me when I asked you. I came home and there was a man on my front porch saying that my dad was very sick. I had to leave in a hurry. I told Mr. Howard where I was and why I was leaving. I figured he'd tell you the next day. You never sent a telegram, a letter, nothing. Not once. So who deserted who, Katy Lynn?"

Something didn't feel right about his story. She crossed her arms over her chest and narrowed her eyes. Giving him the benefit of a doubt, she wondered if he'd asked her to get in touch with him when she was half asleep.

"I tried calling you," he continued. "Then I went to the office and Livvy was about to tell me what hotel you were in, but Marie said you'd explicitly stated you didn't want to be disturbed. The way she said it left no doubt that I was on the top of the list."

"When did you tell me to get in touch with you? Was I awake?" she asked.

"I didn't tell you. I wrote a note and left it on a sofa pillow. Right beside your face. There's no way in the world you could have not seen it, Katy. For a moment I thought about leaving it on the counter in the kitchen, but I wanted it to be the first thing you saw when you opened your eyes. I asked you to get in touch with me as soon as you were awake. I didn't want to wake you, but I had to leave. It just wouldn't have looked right for me to be there when daylight came," he said.

"Yeah, right." She'd heard enough by then. For some twisted, strange reason Joshua was lying to her. Desertion. Lying. Neither could be a stone for building a foundation to support a relationship. "Good-bye Joshua."

"What are you doing, Katy?" he asked in confusion.

"I'm going home. You definitely are Thaddeus Carter's son. You wrote me a note and left it on my pillow just about as surely as there is going to be a heat wave by noon."

She stormed off the porch, leaving Joshua in a state of mass bewilderment. She stomped all the way back to the café only to find Andy already gone. She hitched up her wet skirt tail, hopped up into the buggy, and went straight home where she parked the rig in the stable, rubbed down the horse, and fed him before she went into the house. She threw herself on the settee and tried to make sense of the whole argument where there was none to be found. Finally she drifted off into a fitful sleep borne of several nights of no sleep.

When she awoke it was dark both outside and inside. She reached behind her head and lit the lamp. "Good grief," she muttered. It was already 8:00 and she was starving. She made herself a ham sandwich, poured a glass of milk, and carried them back to the sofa. While she ate she picked up the book she'd been reading and tried to finish the chapter but couldn't keep her mind on it.

She dropped her bookmark when she laid the book aside and carried her plate and glass back to the kitchen. She popped the last bite of sandwich into her mouth and washed what few dishes had accumulated beside the sink, then treated herself to a long, bubble bath. There were stages of mourning. She'd known every one of them after her mother died even though she was just a little girl. She'd repeated them one by one after her father died. And again when she woke up today and realized she'd really, truly lost Joshua. The numbness had arrived. Seven years later than it should have, but it was there when she eased herself down through a thick layer of bubbles into the warm bath. After the numbness came anger and then acceptance, etc.

The warm water and soft-smelling bubbles put her to sleep again. When she awoke, her neck in a bind from falling asleep against the back of the tub, the bubbles were flat and the water chilly. She fished a towel out of the wash stand and hurriedly wrapped herself in it. She padded to her bedroom and pulled on a pair of cotton underpants and her oldest, softest flannel gown. When she brushed her hair she remembered that Andy had given her the brush for Christmas. That and the engraved silver bookmark she'd dropped on the living room floor.

"That's no way to treat a present," she said aloud, and went back to the front of the house to retrieve the bookmark. She got down on her knees and looked beside the table legs. No bookmark. Finally she put her cheek on the floor and looked under the settee and there it was right beside a piece of paper.

She had both a blank piece of paper and the book-mark in her hand when she stood up. She went back to the bedroom and put the marker back in her book and tossed the blank piece of paper into the small trash can beside her desk. Her aim wasn't as good as usual and the paper landed just shy of the can. She picked it up and started to wad it into a ball, so she could at least get it into the can on the second try. She frowned when she noticed writing on the other side of the paper. She un-rumpled the ball she had made and there was the note. The one Joshua said he left on her pillow . . . it must have blown under the sofa before she woke up. Tears welled up in her eyes and rolled down her cheeks in great rivers, dripping on to her gown.

She crammed her feet down into the first pair of shoes she found—old, worn brown work boots she used when she mucked out the stables—but she didn't tie them. She grabbed the long dress coat she'd worn to church that morning from the back of the rocking chair. It was midnight when she finally slung a leg over the side saddle and headed south toward town.

Joshua laced his hands behind his head and stared at a blank ceiling. The sleet had stopped a couple of hours before and the stars were bright. The moon cast its glow through the lace curtains on his bedroom window, mak-ing strange little patterns all over the room. He heard a horse whinny and was out of bed, getting his robe on before he heard the knock. He lit a lamp and opened the door.

Tears were still streaming down Katy Lynn's face when he motioned for her to come inside. Andy must have died. That would be the only reason she would come back to him for anything after the fit she threw that afternoon.

"Joshua," she sobbed, "I am so sorry."

"For what?"

She held up the crumpled piece of paper. "I found it under the sofa. You did write a note and it must have blown under there before I woke up."

He smiled and opened his arms. "I should have left it on the countertop." He whispered between planting kisses on her forehead. "I couldn't understand why you were ignoring me, and now I can understand why you were so angry."

"Shhh," she put her finger on his mouth. "We both know what went wrong. Just hold me Joshua. It's the trusting thing that I'm having trouble with."

"Yes, ma'am," he agreed readily.

He eased her coat off without really letting go and then pushed her back to look at her. A worn flannel gown, untied boots, and a red nose. Her hair hung down her back and he thought she was more beautiful right then than he'd ever seen her before.

He bent down, took her boots off, and picked up his sweet Katy Lynn to carry her across the living room, where he fully well intended to start a fire and cuddle up with her in his arms. "Katy, I'm in love with you. Have been even before I knew what love was."

"Mmmm," she mumbled, returning his kiss.

She awoke with a start at 3:00 in the morning. Surely she hadn't fallen asleep. Joshua pulled her into his embrace and kissed her on the top of her head. "Do you have to go to work? Can't you just this one time send a message to the girls and tell them you are . . ."

". . . sick?" she giggled. "I never felt better in my entire life. Besides Marie is under the weather and isn't coming in today. You go back to sleep, darlin'. You don't have to be on a time schedule. Oh, no, Joshua! What if someone sees me leaving the parsonage at this time of the morning? They'll fire you!"

"No, they won't. I think half the congregation knows I'm in love with you already. And yes, I do have to go to work this morning. I have a group of ladies coming to discuss starting a women's organization," he groaned, working the kinks of his neck. The fire was dead and what little he'd slept had been with Katy curled up tightly in his arms. "Katy what are we going to do about us?"

"Just don't write me a note," she told him. "I'll be home by five o'clock this evening. We can talk then if . . ."

"I'll be there." He kissed her one more time before she rushed out the door.

Chapter Thirteen

Minty-green leaves covered the trees and there was enough lush green grass on the church lawn for an Easter egg hunt on Saturday. On Friday night before the big hunt, Joshua made red dye and pale yellow dye from onion skins, while Katy boiled and cooled dozens and dozens of eggs. With a bit of shaved candle wax, he drew pictures on the eggs before he dipped them. On the last one he created a lovely rose.

"A lovely rose. Perhaps you will find this one," he said, removing the egg from the cup.

The hunt was scheduled for nine-thirty with a brunch in the fellowship hall afterward. Katy was grateful that she didn't have to help prepare that too. She could make gravy if no one minded a few lumps, and she could fry fish and hushpuppies to perfection, but that was the extend of her culinary skills. She'd made a cake once, but Andy couldn't eat it so she'd thrown it out and not even the wild animals would touch it. She'd have to learn to cook someday, but she was glad it wasn't any time soon.

"If I do, I'm keeping it. That is the prettiest one yet. Whatever little girl finds it won't want to crack it open," Katy said.

"Who says some little boy doesn't find it?" Joshua teased.

"Or worse yet—that it's the one that doesn't get found at all. The one that is hid so well that no one finds it until Mrs. Roberts steps on it after Sunday morning services in about six weeks. Then it will be nice and ripe and the yoke will be green. She may leave the church over such an abomination." She giggled.

"Then you and I'd better count every egg before we hide them and do a tally after the children find them. It would be a shame if Mrs. Roberts stepped on one and lost her salvation." He laughed with her. "There. All done. In plenty of time for you to get home and don one of your costumes for your piano playing tonight."

Katy took his hand and led him to the living room. He'd rolled up his shirt sleeves and she could see the scar creeping down his upper arm. She ran her finger along the rough skin and planted a kiss on it before she pulled him down in a rocking chair. She sat in his lap, wrapped her arms around his neck and kissed him. "Will you be there when I get home?"

"Do you want me to be? Which reminds me, Katy.

We've talked about us and gotten the past all worked out now. I can't give up my profession. I made a deal with God and besides I love the ministry. It's my niche in life. But what are you going to do about The Dove, honey?" He ran a fingertip down her cheek bone.

"Why should I do anything about it?"

"Katy, I don't think . . ."

"Are you telling me to give up my saloon?" She drew her dark eyebrows down over eyes that were anything but sweet and happy.

"I'm telling you that I'm a liberal thinker, but I don't think you should be playing until two o'clock in the morning before Sunday morning services."

"Has it ever kept me from making it to church before?" she argued even though the same issue had been on her mind for weeks and weeks.

"Are we having a fight?"

"I'm not fighting. I'm going home. I've got to get ready for tonight." She jumped off his lap and headed for the door.

"Katy, think about it for a while," he said. Mercy, but a life with that girl was definitely going to be a bed of roses . . . complete with big, sticky thorns. He'd told her he loved her and the only thing keeping him from actually proposing was that blasted saloon. Until she saw the light and realized a minister's wife couldn't play the piano in a saloon, even if it was a classy joint, any thoughts of marriage were just as concrete as whistling Dixie in the middle of a tornado.

"Okay, I'll think about it," she said curtly as she

picked up her purse and left, without even stopping to look back.

She rushed around, scrubbing dye from her hands, and putting her hair up. Then she flipped through her costumes, fingering each one of them lovingly. The red dress was what she'd worn that first night. It was the flashiest, most daring one she owned and it represented the days when The Dove was first finished. The bright blue was next in line. Made that the next summer when Andy suggested she should have more than one dress to wear. Blue, with black trim, like what most folks thought of when they conjured up a mental picture of a barmaid.

She went through them one by one and then decided on the red one for that night. She'd started her career at The Dove in that dress. It seemed only fitting after the argument with Joshua that she should wear it that night—a soiled dove doing her job. She piled her hair high on her head and kept her chin high as she walked from her front door to the back door of the roadhouse.

"Red tonight?" Andy looked up and dusted off the bar with a damp cloth.

"Yes, red for anger. Joshua started in on me tonight about The Dove, Andy. He doesn't think I should play here anymore. Why shouldn't I? He sure hasn't asked me to marry him. Maybe he's satisfied with status quo. Maybe I am too. Until I'm a preacher's wife, I'm just another woman and he sure doesn't have the right to tell me what to do," she said.

"Who are you trying to convince? Me or you? Seems

you been trying to do that a lot these past few months. Talking to me but trying to convince yourself."

"Whose side are you on?" she snapped at him.

"Yours of course. Whose side are you on?"

"What's that supposed to mean?"

"You haven't been content here in a while Katy Lynn, and you know it." He shook the rag at her while he talked. "Not since the time when you went out with Joshua that Wednesday night. The customers don't know any difference, but I sure do. There's wistfulness in your blue eyes like you'd rather be somewhere else."

"Andy!"

"I'm only blind in one eye. The other one sees just fine," he said. "I know you two belong together. And this roadhouse is standing between you two and that's a pure crying shame. It's just a building and it's just a job. If it's more important than what makes your heart sing, then you've got more of your mother's blood than I would have ever believed."

"You're sure on a soapbox." She sat down at the piano and began to play. Andy was right. Her heart wasn't in it and she would have rather been curled up in Joshua's arms than sitting there in all her finery warming up for the evening.

"I am on a soapbox, too, and I'm not ready to get off it yet," she said.

Andy pulled up a chair and sat down beside her. "Then let's have it out, my child. We've argued. We've laughed and cried together. If I'd had a daughter of my own I would have wanted her to be just like you, Katy

Lynn. I've got a solution to this problem. I understand the church needs a new piano. Donate this one to it and let me run this place."

"But Andy, I like playing," she said.

"Play for the church if you like playing that much. I know the lady who plays would gladly step down . . ."

"And just how do you know that?" She stopped abruptly and stared at him.

"Because I've been keeping company with her daughter," he chuckled. "About three months now and she told me so. Anyway, I'd like to open the roadhouse on Thursday, Friday, and Saturday. Close it up the first of the week because we hardly make enough to open the doors then. I'd keep it closed on Sundays because I ain't going to flirt with my luck on that one. I'll share the profits even up like always, but I'd like to live in your house once you move to the parsonage. Also the lady I've been keeping company with used to do a little bit of piano playing at a joint down in Bowie. I might hire her to help me and I'll pay her out of my profits."

"You must've stayed up nights to get all this figured out. But you are full of bull. You'll pay her out of the earnings and then we'll split the profits. And you can only live in my house when and if Joshua Carter asks me to marry him. You're not about to move in with me. We'd kill each other in a week."

Andy threw back his head and roared. "Girl, you're going to have a job of it. A preacher's wife? Your mother would turn over in her grave and your daddy's old chest would just plumb swell up in pride. But that temper has got to go."

"My temper won't ever go. I'll buy the church a new piano. They wouldn't want one that came out of this place," she said.

"Nope, I want this one out of here. If it's still in the corner, it'll draw you back and it will make you and Joshua fight even more. Use your money to have a new pulpit made for Joshua to stand behind and everyone will be so busy looking at it that they won't see the piano. Besides it sits back in a corner, don't it?"

"You've got all the answers, don't you?" She cocked her head to one side.

"I've been working on the questions while you've been playing."

"So when does this arrangement begin?"

"Right now. The movers are coming to take the piano out on Monday morning. The carpenters will have the new pulpit done the same day. Solid oak with all kinds of fancy work done on it, including an engraved cross on the front. It will be in the church the same day. Right now you're going to play "Amazing Grace" for me and go home," he said.

"But, I can't walk away like that. I need time to adjust. How about I finish tonight and tomorrow night and then just play one time next week? Besides"—she realized what he'd done behind her back—"just what gave you the right to make plans before you even asked me about it? We're a team. We've been a team since I was born and you've gone and . . ."

"Katy, the team will always be there, but you added a third member. I'm your father, your mother, your friend and uncle, and everything else. But he's the love of your life. The plans could all be undone if you don't like them. But you need to make a clean break. Get up and walk out of here. Go back to Joshua and tell that fine young man you took care of a building and a piano, and you'll take care of anything else that comes between you in the next sixty years. Anything worth having is worth fighting for, even if you have to fight your own self."

She bowed her head for a minute. Andy was right, but it wasn't going to be easy to give up or to give in. She reached across the space between them and hugged him tightly. "I don't know that I've ever said this before, Andy, but I love you."

"Posh," he hugged her again. "Body don't have to say what's down deep in their heart and I knew you loved me first time I saw you. And that's when I fell in love with you, girl."

She nodded.

Words would bring on a whole bevy of tears. She simply sat back down and played "Amazing Grace" and then calmly walked out the back door.

Joshua lined the baskets of eggs up on the table and decided he wouldn't go sit in the shadows at The Dove that night. She could walk home alone or Andy could take her. They needed some thinking time and a couple of days would be good for them. He was about to lock the front door when it flew open and his mother and father swept inside, telling him they'd driven up for the weekend so they could be there for the holiday festivities.

"Well, this is a surprise," he said, "Katy and I've worked on eggs all day so they're everywhere but come in and I'll make a pot of coffee."

"Katy was here in the parsonage?" Thaddeus asked gruffly as Ruth carried their satchel down the hall to the spare bedroom.

"Dad, I'm in love with Katy Lynn Logan. I haven't made a secret of it," he said bluntly and then wondered if he was itching for a fight with someone since Katy had run out on him without finding a solution to their problem.

"You were in love with that trashy girl years ago. That's why I sent you away and paid her off. I didn't want to give her word back to her, but your mother laid down the law and threatened to leave me. Katy sent the money back with interest, but that doesn't mean for one minute I'm ever going to like her. She's not preacher's wife material, son. Remember your position and what's best for your people."

"She sent back the money *with interest*?"

"Yes, but it won't buy back her reputation, Joshua. You'll be getting trash if you don't wake up and you'll never have a bigger church than this one." Thaddeus' voice was filled with acid.

"I don't feel that way. I feel like she's the most precious jewel in the lot and I don't care about a bigger church. I'll be content right here in Spanish Fort the rest of my life if I can have Katy," Joshua said.

"A pearl in a pig's snout." Thaddeus quoted part of a scripture. "If you marry her I'll . . ."

"You won't do one thing, Thaddeus," Ruth said softly. "That woman is a pearl all right, but there's not a hog in sight. Now I'll hear no more from you. I've got a cake and I'll make the coffee. Joshua, would you please go take our rig out to the stable and put it away. I'll have things all ready for a visit when you finish."

He pulled on a sweater and buttoned it up the front, ignored the black cloud hanging around Thaddeus, and opened the door to find Katy standing before him in her red costume. Big tears rolled down her cheeks like they did the night she brought his crumpled note in her hand to apologize. He stepped outside and opened his arms and without a word she melted into them. This was where she belonged. In Joshua's arms and if he was content with the way things were, then she would have to convince him that she wanted more.

"What's going on, Katy?" He pushed her back just enough to look down into her crystal-clear blue eyes, which were glimmering with something between sadness and elation.

"Andy solved our problem."

"The Dove problem, or the green egg and Mrs. Robert's soul?" He smiled.

"You know. He's going to run the business for me and I'll still have my share of the profits. And he's got a lady friend who might play the piano."

"Are you content with this?" he asked. Twenty years down the road he didn't want to wake up one morning to find that Katy had changed her mind.

"The soiled dove has come home." She laid her head back on his chest. "She would like for you to take her home now and kiss her one last time before she takes this costume off for the last time. It seems only fitting that you be the one to kiss away the dirt from off her wings, doesn't it?"

He scooped her up, loaded her into her buggy and drove her home. They could hear the Victrola playing loudly and the customers' laughter as he carried her across the threshold into her house, but neither one drew Katy's heart through the back door. All she could think about was Joshua.

"How did you know I'd be back?" She asked when he set her down in the living room.

"What are you talking about?"

"The buggy. It just dawned on me. There was a buggy there, parked beside your house with the horses all ready. And you were going in the house. Had you been somewhere?"

"Mother and Father had just arrived. I was going out the door to put the rig away but then something more important came up," he hugged her closely.

She rolled up on her tiptoes to kiss him. "I see. They'll think it took you an extra long time to put that rig away by the time you get back to town."

"I'll saddle up your horse and ride him back. Can Andy bring you tomorrow?"

"Yes, he can. And Andy says the piano is moving to the church . . . on Monday."

"That piano in the church?" he sputtered.

"Yep. Just how liberal are you?"

"We need a new piano. But that one?" he asked with a bewildered look. "Why did Andy think of that and how did he know?"

"It's a long story," she said.

"We've got to start hiding eggs early, but the night is young. Is that long enough for you to tell it?"

She grinned. "Andy is seeing a woman who is the daughter of our pianist, who wants to resign and let me play in the church, according to Andy. Anyway he says if the piano is at The Dove it will draw me back to it. He probably thinks it will call out to me wherever it is and if it's in the church . . ."

"He's a wise man, but . . ."

"No buts, the moving men will put it in the church on Monday. Right after the carpenters get there with a brand new pulpit for you so the piano won't stand out like a sore thumb. And I suppose the next Sunday I'll have to start playing."

"Andy is a wise man. Remind me to thank him," he said.

She kicked playfully at his shin. "Andy is a wise man? I'm the one making this big new change. So . . ."

"Thank you, then," Joshua said, "my little peace dove."

"Good grief, where did that come from?" She snarled her nose at the mushy name. "I'm the soiled dove, not a peace dove."

"Not anymore. The soiled dove is gone. You are now a peace dove because you've brought peace to my life, Katy Lynn."

"Don't say that very often." She giggled. "I don't want to try to live up to that name. I've been the soiled dove for so long, the change might undo me. Besides it sounds like something a snuff-dipping dirt farmer would call his wife. One who has five kids hanging on her skirt tails and lives in a shack."

Joshua laughed. "I'm going home now, Katy Lynn. Want to go with me? Mother and Father are there, but I'm sure Mother would be glad to see you."

She kissed him passionately then pushed him out the door. "No, thank you. The parsonage isn't big enough for me and Thaddeus both."

Chapter Fourteen

"Has he proposed yet?" Livvy asked when Katy walked through the door a week later. "I'm sure not looking forward to dancing a jig in a pig trough, and James is pressuring me to set a date." She held out her finger and the diamond ring glittered in the sunlight streaming in the east window.

"You better start practicing." Katy laughed. "We got The Dove problem finalized. The piano is in the church."

". . . and the pulpit is lovely," Marie said.

"Andy was right. It *has* created more talk than the piano," Katy said.

"I hate to bring this up ladies, but we need to have a conference. A real important one so I put the closed sign on the door. As of now we are closed for an hour," Marie grinned apologetically.

"Oh?" Katy tilted her chin down and looked up at them.

"Yes." Livvy cleared her throat. "Let's get it laid out on the table."

"Oh, no," Katy whined. "It's about the business and you two promised me you'd never change your minds."

They pulled up three chairs around a table and Katy's heart fell to her knees. First The Dove and now SD Enterprises. She didn't know if she could endure it. Even if Andy was right and she shouldn't let anything keep her from Joshua.

"I've got it pretty well planned out, but I'm open for suggestions." Marie opened a folder. "I'll put my two cents in first and then you two can chip right in when you are ready. I don't want to leave the business, but I want some free time for Davy and me. I sure don't want to quit making money. Even if he does say he's rich as Midas, he doesn't have an inkling of what I'm worth on the books. So what I propose is this. We each work a two day week. I'll work Monday and Tuesday. Livvy can have Wednesday and Thursday. Katy can have Friday and Saturday. The next week Livvy gets Monday and Tuesday, Katy gets Wednesday and Thursday, and I pick up Friday and Saturday. That way one of us doesn't always get the Saturday. This can all be flexible. We will hire a full-time clerk and we'll each take two whole weeks off in the summertime. During that time the remaining two will each pick up an extra day," Marie said.

"If we need to, we could hire two full-time clerks. We can afford it," Livvy said.

"What if Joshua does propose and then he gets assigned to a church off in Oklahoma or Arkansas?" Katy asked.

"You can come back once a month on the railroad for a conference. It will all work itself out," Livvy said. "None of us want to quit, but we all want a little more free time to enjoy the finer things in life."

"So what do you think?" Marie sipped her coffee.

"I think you saved a whole morning in vain," Katy said. "Go turn the sign around and tell the town we are open again."

"Then you like my proposal?" Marie asked.

"I love it," Livvy said. "Can I have my two weeks vacation in June? Davy says we'll go to New York for our honeymoon."

"So even if Joshua does get his feet out of cold water and propose, I need to schedule a wedding for . . .? I think your words were that I would beat you to the altar and if I didn't you would dance a jig in a pig trough at mine," Katy teased. But deep down she was beginning to wonder if she was going to have to do the asking. Joshua seemed pretty satisfied with the arrangement they had now that she wasn't playing the piano at The Dove.

"You better get that man in gear and set it up for May. Someone as tall and gangly as me dancing a jig in a pig trough in her wedding dress would be too, too much, Katy Lynn Logan. I'd fall and break my neck and poor old James would be heartbroken. Now, seriously, I'd like to get this two-day-a-week thing started real soon. Like this week," Livvy said.

"Okay," Katy said. "Let's call it a deal. Marie, since you came up with most of this idea, do you have someone in mind to hire or do we make a Help Wanted sign for the front window?"

"Actually, I do. Miz Raven's daughter, Susanna, knows the place and I think she'd be a wonderful clerk. She's quiet spoken, pretty as a picture, and really smart. I'd like to talk to her about the job before we put out a sign. She might also have a friend who'd be interested in working with her."

"And someday when we're ready to sell our store, she and her friend will buy it. Maybe they won't even need an Andy when it's their turn to take over the reins," Livvy said.

"I'm not ready to give up the ghost and sell the store just yet," Katy said. "But Susanna would be a good choice if she's interested. Hey, I just want to say I'm glad you two didn't abandon me. I've been scared to death you'd forsake me."

"And all those wonderful SD dollars. I don't think so." Livvy laughed. "If Joshua doesn't propose by the first of May, I plan to have a talk with him myself. I'm not dancing in a pig trough at my own wedding."

"Don't you dare talk to Joshua. If this is ever going to work, it has to be because he truly loves me and wants me to be his wife, not because you held a gun to his head."

"I don't own a gun. But I do have a really sharp knife." Livvy laughed on her way out of the office.

Joshua was waiting on the porch when she got home that evening. A basket with a red-checkered cover was sitting beside him, along with two fishing poles. His work pants were frayed at the legs and he wore an old straw fishing hat with hooks stuck on the brim.

Katy thought he was the most handsome man she'd ever laid eyes on. She wrapped her arms around his neck and pulled his face down for a long, passionate kiss.

"Fishing or kissing," she whispered in his ear.

His heart skipped a couple of beats. Would she always affect him like that?

"I think you better go shuck out of those pretty business clothes and put on a pair of your old worn-out overalls. Andy told me the catfish are hitting today and I bet we can get enough for a fish fry. Maybe even invite Andy and his new lady friend. Her name is Molly, in case you haven't met her. A fifty-year-old lady with long blond hair and the prettiest green eyes you've ever seen. She thinks Andy hung the moon and stars."

"You have a doubt that he didn't? And how on earth did you find out her age? Did you have to sell your soul? Women don't tell their age."

"Her mother told me her age and that she's not real happy she's took up with someone in the saloon business. I won't touch that comment about Andy. I thought I hung them where you are concerned. I've got sandwiches and cookies. Get a move on it, lady. We're wasting time," he said.

"And who hung the moon and stars for you?" she asked.

"What?" He'd already lost the conversation thread.

"The moon and stars?"

"Oh, this dove tossed them up there one night back when I was fishing on the river. Got them in the right place on the first try," he said.

"You are a hopeless romantic." She planted a kiss on his cheek and then hurried down the hallway toward her bedroom.

They carried the basket, her famous old quilt, and the poles through the trees to the riverbank where they set up camp and tossed their lines out into the murky waters. Joshua's palms were clammy. He'd tried a dozen times to ask her to marry him but always got cold feet at the last moment. He couldn't shake her hand after church services and say, "Katy Lynn Logan, will you marry me," and then go on to the next person in line while she thought about it.

One thing that could be written in stone, as Katy often said, was that he'd never have a humdrum life with his dove—peace or soiled. She would keep him on his toes right up until he drew his last breath.

"Katy, what are you going to do if I die before you?"

"What in the devil brought that question on?" she asked.

"I was just thinking about life."

"Well, I suppose I'd need about three days to get my

affairs in order. That's all the time they'd give you to wait at the gates, and the only way I'll ever get into heaven, darlin', is riding on your coattails. Then I'd die so I could join you and you could sneak me in and we could spend eternity together." She felt tension. What on earth could he be thinking about? Had he found he only had a little while to live? Her heart crawled up in her throat and she thought she was going to be sick. Life without Joshua, now that she'd found him? She couldn't bear it. She might really die.

"Why are you asking?" she finally whispered when she found her voice again. "You're not seriously sick are you?"

"No," he shook his head.

She let out a double lungful of air. "Then don't you ever scare me like that again, or I'll kick you out in the middle of that river and leave you there," she snapped.

He reeled in the bobble and laid the rod on the bank, and pulled her close to his side. "I love you, Katy Lynn. I've tried every way in the world to say this for a month and it just wouldn't come out right. I wanted to take you somewhere very romantic. So I thought why not go back to the beginning. Back to where I really met you for the first time all those years ago. It was right here on this very spot. And it was here that I left you at the end of that summer, so I decided to come back here to talk about this. Katy, I'm a preacher. I don't make a lot of money. At least not a lot compared to what you make and that's not been easy for me to swallow. But I have gotten past part of that man-must-earn-the-living stuff and realized that you are a very intelligent woman with a lot of power and business sense." Joshua stopped and she waited.

"Is this a proposal?"

"No, but this is." He tilted her chin back and kissed her until they were both breathless. "I love you with my whole heart and soul and I'm asking you to be my wife, Katy Lynn."

"Then the answer is yes." She smiled.

"What about your job? What if I get moved? What if . . ."

She kissed his eyelids, his nose, his mouth and tried to chase away the fears that had been plaguing her for weeks also. "The what if's are taken care of already," she finally whispered. "We had a conference at work and it's taken care of."

"When can we get married and make this legal?"

"Anytime you want," she said.

"You mean it? I want you to sit on the front pew when I preach. I want to introduce you as my wife. I want to take you home for Mother's Day," he said.

"Oh no! What are we going to do about Thaddeus?"

"You take care of your job situation so I don't have to worry about that end of it, and I'll take care of Dad."

"Then let's get married on the first day of May. At the courthouse with Andy and Mr. Howard for witnesses. Andy won't be able to walk me down the aisle if we get married at the courthouse, but he could be at the wedding, and then a honeymoon somewhere very private. The church can have a reception when we return."

"Sure you don't want the big thing with Livvy and Marie for bridesmaids?" he asked.

"I love you so much, Joshua. I just want to be your wife. I don't need a big wedding to be that."

"Married with no fanfare it is. Bet Andy changes your mind," he said.

"I bet Thaddeus changes yours. You may be hunting a job next week," she said right back.

"Are we fighting? Wait a minute," he said in stunned silence. "I forgot." He pulled a velvet box from the pocket of his jeans and popped it open to reveal a diamond solitaire set on a gold band.

"It's beautiful." She kissed his fingertips and held up her own hand. "Put it on my hand and we'll have good luck forever."

Chapter Fifteen

Katy Lynn couldn't believe it was already the first of May or that she'd actually let Andy talk her into a church wedding. She looked at the dress hanging from a hook in the ceiling of the Sunday school room—a frothy white concoction that made Marie's wedding dress look very plain. But Andy and his new lady friend, Molly, along with Livvy and Marie had all trooped out to The Paradise, Miz Raven's place, and sat around a table while she drew up the plans. They'd all had their say-so by the time the morning was finished and in two weeks Miz Raven had the dress finished.

The small wedding of only four grew to a few church folks who told a few more and now the whole congregation had been invited and the church packed. Andy loved it and Molly, bless her heart, had bought a mother's dress in pale blue crepe.

"Time to get you ready." Livvy swept into the room. She and Marie wore light-blue satin dresses and would carry an arm bouquet of lilies caught up with a wide satin ribbon in navy.

"I can not believe I let the bunch of you talk me into this." She snorted. "I wanted four people and a judge and look at this monstrosity. Flowers all over the church and candles everywhere. And that dress? There's not room for another pin tuck or piece of lace. Even Marie didn't do this kind of hoopla."

"Marie didn't marry the preacher. This isn't your day, darlin', it's the church's and Andy's day. Tonight belongs to you. Sure you don't want to tell me where you are going?" she teased as she helped Katy into the dress and buttoned her sleeves.

"No, you just better be glad I'm getting married this afternoon and not in July. You got out of that pig trough thing pretty easy," Katy said.

"But you still owe me money," Marie reminded her.

"Money is in your purse. I stuck it in there just minutes ago. I never go back on a good solid bet," Katy said.

"Can I come in?" Ruth opened the door. "Oh, look at you, Katy. You are so lovely. Joshua is fairly well beaming. I can not tell you how happy I am to finally have a daughter and the prospect of grandchildren."

Katy blushed scarlet red. Livvy stifled a giggle. Marie coughed to cover up her chuckle.

"Well, I hope that later part takes a little while," Katy said.

"I don't," Ruth said. "I wouldn't even care if it was one of those instant babies."

"What?" Marie asked.

"You know, the old saying from years ago. The first one can get here anytime. Six months from the wedding day, seven months, even two months. All the rest take nine months to hatch."

"Ruth!" Katy exclaimed.

"Well, I wouldn't. I'm ready for grandchildren," she said stoically. "There's the music and that's my cue. Time to seat the mothers. I think it's really sweet of you to include Molly. I understand Andy has been special to you all your life and she's so excited about today. I just wanted to sneak a peek at you and I'm surely not disappointed. You are truly lovely and I'm blessed to be getting you for a daughter. I shall look forward to having you and Joshua on Mother's Day weekend."

"Thank you, and Ruth, there's not an instant baby on the way," Katy said.

"Oh, my." Marie burst into giggles when she was gone.

"Hush. Let's go girls. Andy will be waiting." Katy was still blushing when she picked up her bouquet of fresh cut roses laid in a bed of soft weeping willow branches with streaming satin ribbons.

She peeped around the edge of the door and watched Livvy stroll down the aisle. The church was full. Joshua waited at the front with Mr. Howard and another deacon beside him. Thaddeus looked like he would actually dance a jig in a muddy hog wallow if Katy dropped dead half way down the aisle. She hadn't asked Joshua what he did to get his father to perform the ceremony. She really didn't want to know.

Marie followed Livvy and then it was time for Katy and Andy. He puffed his chest out and patted her hand looped through his arm. "It's our turn, baby. Your momma and daddy would be proud to see this day. But not any prouder than I am. Let's knock 'em dead, darlin'."

"You bet we will," she whispered. "We are a team."

She stepped into the doorway and everyone else in the room disappeared when Joshua's heart and hers met somewhere in the middle of the church. Andy said the right words when Thaddeus asked who was in charge of giving her away, and then Joshua took her hand and that old familiar jolt was there.

"We are gathered here today to join my son, Joshua Thomas Carter, in holy matrimony with Katherine Lyndsey Logan. Marriage is a holy estate . . ." he intoned beautifully, his deep voice reminding Katy of Joshua's preaching voice. But there was another voice that Joshua had, even deeper and softer. A voice that belonged to her alone. He swore she'd put her own special brand on him years before, but as they exchanged their vows and rings before a whole church full of people she knew beyond a shadow that it was now hers for all eternity.

"By the authority vested in me by God and the states of Oklahoma and Texas, I now pronounce you man and wife." Thaddeus ended the ceremony traditionally. "Joshua you may kiss your bride."

The reception was an even bigger affair than the wedding, with tables filled with enough food to feed an army of hungry harvesters, according to Ruth. Joshua and Katy cut the five-tiered cake with love birds on the top and fed each other. They locked arms and drank punch from engraved goblets. A photographer recorded the cutting of the cake and took a picture of the bride and groom together.

"My eyes are blurry," she whispered to Joshua.

"I shall kiss the blurriness away when we get to our private train car." He leaned down to brush butterfly kisses across her eyelids.

"Much more of that and I'll seduce you in the Sunday school room," she told him.

"We are married now so it would be legal, but I couldn't guarantee it wouldn't be interrupted. Your punch glass is empty. Let me go refill it, darling," he said.

As soon as he left, Thaddeus appeared at her elbow. "This is not a happy beginning and I'm not going to say I've had a change of heart and like you, Katy Lynn Logan. I still think you are a soiled dove."

"I'd say that we are probably in agreement," she smiled brightly at Joshua coming across the room. "I don't imagine I'm going to wake up tomorrow and like you either. But we both love Joshua so who knows, some day we might be able to tolerate each other for his sake. And Preacher Carter, I will always be a soiled dove. I shall work very hard to always be just that. Because that's what Joshua fell in love with in the very beginning of our relationship, and I wouldn't change that for anything. Hello, darling." She looked up at Joshua who had a worried look on his face. "Your dad and I were just having a little visit. Thank you for the punch. Are you ready to go now?" She took the cup of punch from Joshua and handed it to Thaddeus.

"Yes, ma'am."

"Then excuse us, Daddy Carter," she said sweetly. "We are looking forward to seeing you on Mother's Day weekend. Ya'll be careful driving home."

Thaddeus set his jaw to keep from grinning. That vixen was going to make them all toe the line and he might like her after all, but he'd be double hanged if he ever let her know it.

The sun, barely a sliver of an orange ball on the horizon, cast a glow through the window of the train car. Tomorrow they'd be somewhere on a small island with no one around for a whole week. She'd said they would take the train to south Texas and a ferry out to the island. He didn't care if Katy's money paid for the honeymoon. He just wanted a whole week with her in his arms.

He carried her over the threshold, straight to the bed, and laid her down gently on the feather pillow. A single lamp had been lit. A light supper was laid on the table and the bed turned down already. "I love you," he said for the hundredth time that day as he stretched out beside her.

"And I love you, Joshua. Since I first laid eyes on you, I've loved you," she snuggled deeply into his shoulder. "Promise you'll never leave me again."

"I promise," he said, giving her a lingering kiss that convinced her.

WITHDRAWN

F BRO
Brown, Carolyn,
The dove /

FORT RECOVERY PUBLIC LIBRARY

Ⓑ

S. f